Red Velvet and Revenge

A Peridale Cafe MYSTERY

AGATHA FROST

ALSO BY AGATHA FROST

The Peridale Café Series
Pancakes and Corpses
Lemonade and Lies
Doughnuts and Deception
Chocolate Cake and Chaos
Shortbread and Sorrow
Espresso and Evil
Macarons and Mayhem
Fruit Cake and Fear
Birthday Cake and Bodies
Gingerbread and Ghosts
Cupcakes and Casualties
Blueberry Muffins and Misfortune
Ice Cream and Incidents
Champagne and Catastrophes
Wedding Cake and Woes
Red Velvet and Revenge
Vegetables and Vengeance

The Scarlet Cove Series
Dead in the Water
Castle on the Hill
Stroke of Death

A Peridale Cafe MYSTERY

Book Sixteen

1

"It's snowing again," Julia told Barker as she set a fresh cup of coffee next to his antique typewriter in the dining room of their Peridale cottage. "And to think, we're already in February."

"*Huh*?" Barker grunted, fingers still pounding on the heavy keys.

"More snow." Julia nodded at the window behind him. "It's February."

"*February*?" Barker frowned, eyes still trained

on the paper. "Since when?"

"Since three days ago."

"Right, yeah. Of course."

"Not that you've been out of this room much recently." Julia eyed the collection of empty coffee cups that had accumulated amongst the masses of paper on the dining room table. "I'm starting to worry about you, Barker."

"Mm-hmm."

"Are you even listening to me?"

"What?"

"*Hello*?" Julia clicked her fingers in front of his face. "Earth to my husband? I know he's in there somewhere."

Barker tore his eyes away from his work and peered up at Julia, his gaze strained. He blinked as though he'd been in another world since before she'd entered the room to replenish his caffeine supply. Dark circles framed his eyes, confirming Julia's suspicions that he hadn't joined her in bed at any point during the night; he looked a decade older.

"I'm sorry, love." Barker ran his hands down his face, his fingers grating against the thick stubble that had come in along his cheeks and jaw. "You have my full attention. What were you saying?"

"I'm worried about you." Julia took the seat next to him and clutched his hands in her own. "You're working yourself into the ground. When was the last time you went outside?"

"Outside?" Barker glanced over his shoulder at their snow-covered back garden as more fluffy flakes drifted from the hazy clouds. "Erm..."

"It was *ten* days ago."

"It was?" Barker's stubbly cheeks blushed maroon.

"Do you even know what day it is?"

"Tuesday?"

"*Sunday.*" Julia chuckled. "See what I mean?"

Barker sighed at his typewriter. "Maybe you have a point, but I don't feel like I have much choice at the moment. Look at the changes they want me to make." He picked up his second novel's manuscript and flicked through to reveal the masses of red pen cluttering every page. "They practically want me to rewrite the entire thing! There isn't a single scene they don't want me to work on. And it's not just small changes either. They're changing the entire story, characters included. If I'd known it would be like this, I would never have left the police force to pursue this stupid fantasy of being an author."

"Oh, Barker." Julia ran her hand along his shoulders. "It's not a fantasy. Your first novel was such a huge hit! You must have made the publishers a small fortune from the sales. They should trust your vision more."

"Well, yesterday's hit is tomorrow's bargain-bin fodder." Barker grabbed his phone and showed Julia a picture of a basket piled high with paperback copies of his first novel, *The Girl in the Basement*. "Someone tweeted me that yesterday. Look at the price! One whole British pound! Is that all I'm worth now? A sole bestseller before I fade into obscurity with the rest of them? I'm the definition of a one-hit wonder. They should call me Barker Bargain-Bin Brown from now on."

"I think the nickname needs more work," she said playfully. "You're not going to fade into obscurity."

"You have to say that," he said with a weary smile, his tired eyes crinkling at the corners, "you're my wife."

Julia continued to rub his back while silence filled the room. They had been married for a little over a month, not that they had been able to enjoy it much. The panicked emails from Barker's publishers had started immediately after Christmas, and since then, Barker had been spending more and more time shut away in the dining room, pounding away on his laptop, and then his typewriter when his eyes couldn't take the strain anymore. Julia hadn't minded indefinitely postponing their honeymoon so he could work on his novel, but she was starting to miss her husband's company.

"I don't feel like I'm getting anywhere." He dropped his head low, his voice faint. "I rewrite the scenes as they ask, but they're never satisfied. They want to drive me crazy, and it's working."

"Is there nothing you can do?"

"Not unless there's a way to get me out of my three-book deal with Mystery Triangle Publishing." He reached out with a shaky hand and picked up his coffee cup. "I should have paid more attention to the small print. Turns out, I'm legally required to provide *at least* one approved manuscript every twelve months from the start of the contract, and those twelve months reset whenever a book is released. That was easy with the first one. They took it as it was written with minimal changes. I never expected them to get so involved. To make things worse, they've already given me my advance, and most of that went into the wedding. For months, the pre-order has been online for an April release to match the first book. They've got me against a wall!"

"That's not fair."

"'Publishing isn't fair', or so my agent keeps reminding me." Barker slurped his coffee, his eyes glazing over as he stared through the paper sticking out of his typewriter. "They keep throwing how much they did for the first release in my face. The press, the TV interviews ... it's like they want me to grovel with gratitude for their generosity." He grimaced. "Maybe I should scrap it and start again? They said they loved the idea of murderous drag queens living in a Blackpool B&B by the sea, and yet they've made changes to every story decision I've made. It *was* based on a true story, *our* true story, but now it barely resembles any ounce of what really happened. I'm beginning to think I'm not cut out for this career."

"You're a *brilliant* writer," Julia assured him. "And I'm sure your second book is just as good as the first. If you'd let me read it, I could try to help?"

"What's the point?" Barker ripped the paper out of the machine, scrunched it up, and tossed it into the corner to join the sea of similar crumpled rejects on the dining room floor. "Nothing I do can save this. I might as well hand back my advance and go crawling to the station. Perhaps they'll take me back as a desk sergeant. Or maybe a cleaner? I must have been going through a mid-life crisis when I quit. Who does that in their thirties after spending so many years becoming a DI?"

Julia squeezed his shoulder reassuringly. Even though she could hear the sarcasm in his voice, the tangible fear in his eyes told her he really thought losing his new career was a possibility. Barker had always dreamed of being a writer. To see his dream twisted before his eyes crushed Julia. The stress he was enduring made running her café feel like child's play.

"Enough about my failures." Barker held back a yawn before clapping his hands together. "What are you doing today? Another lazy Sunday at home while the snow falls outside? We could curl up in front of the fire and watch a film? I need a break from all this."

"I wish I could, I do, but I agreed to judge the Peridale Bake Off, remember?"

"That's today?"

"Sunday the third." Julia nodded as she checked her watch. "Speaking of which, my second batch of cupcakes should be ready to come out."

Leaving Barker in the dining room, Julia hurried into the kitchen and pulled open the oven door. After a quick poke to ensure her cupcakes were cooked through, she placed the hot tray on a cooling rack.

"They smell delicious," Barker remarked as he drifted into the kitchen.

"Ginger and raspberry." Julia tugged off her oven mitts and moved to the first batch, which was now cool enough to decorate. "And here we have lemon and Earl Grey tea. A recipe I perfected last week in the café. Jessie thinks it tastes 'rank', but I'm quite taken by it."

"Speaking of the devil, where is Jessie?" Barker asked as he reached out to grab one of the cupcakes.

"No idea." Julia slapped his hand away. "There aren't enough for spares. I only made thirty, what with the snow carrying on as it has. I doubt the turnout will be what they're expecting."

"Oh, I don't know." Barker climbed onto a stool at the breakfast bar and watched Julia work. "Didn't you say they've got that famous fella judging with you? The one who does the afternoon show on *Cotswold Classic Radio*?"

"Tony Bridges."

"That's him." Barker snapped his fingers. "He comes across like a real down-to-earth guy. We always used to have him on in the station."

"He's all people have been talking about at the café since the announcement in the paper." Julia added buttercream to the final cupcake before applying candied lemon slices on top. "When word spread that I was judging the bake-off with him, people assumed I must know him. I've had everyone from Shilpa to Evelyn asking me to get autographs. They all seemed rather disappointed when I said I'd never met the man. To tell you the truth, I'm not sure I should have agreed to do this in the first place. Who am I to judge people's baking skills?"

"You're the best baker in Peridale, and everyone thinks so." Barker sent her a wink. "There's no one more qualified in the whole county to judge a bake-off, and you know it."

Julia suppressed her smile. Even though she didn't want to admit it openly, she'd been beyond flattered when the Cotswold Baking Society had approached her to judge the first-ever Peridale Bake Off competition. She didn't care that they were barely paying her, or that she'd been asked to provide cupcakes for the coffee and cake hour during the competition, she was just proud they thought she was good enough to take on such a responsibility.

"Does Tony bake?" Barker muttered through a mouthful of buttercream as he piped the leftovers directly into his mouth. "I can't imagine he has much time with a daily radio show."

"I have no idea." Julia shrugged. "He must do if he's agreed to be a judge. I doubt they're paying him much. It's only a small local competition. If he doesn't love baking why else would he get involved? Especially given his allergy."

"Allergy?"

"Peanuts," Julia said, for what felt like the hundredth time that week. "Deathly allergic, according to the organisers. It's been all over the flyers, and I've been reminding people all week not to include any peanuts in their bakes. The last thing we want to do is kill a beloved local celebrity. We don't have all that many to begin with. I can only think of one other."

"Who?"

"A national best-selling author." Julia cupped Barker's face between her palms. "I heard his second novel is coming out soon, and I'm sure it's going to exceed everyone's expectations." She kissed him on the lips. "You can try one of the cupcakes. And when I say one, I mean *one*. I'm going to call Jessie to see where she is. She was gone before I woke up."

Leaving Barker in the kitchen to sample a lemon and Earl Grey cupcake, Julia walked into the sitting room and unplugged her mobile phone from its charger. Perching on the sofa next to Mowgli, who was curled up asleep, she pressed her phone against her ear and cast her gaze through the steamy windows to the sea of white beyond.

The dial tone beeped three times before redirecting to voicemail. Julia might not have been the most technologically savvy person in the village, but she knew that meant Jessie had purposefully rejected her call.

"Jessie, it's Mum," Julia said after a robotic voice instructed her to speak. "Where are you? Don't forget the bake-off. You said you'd be there to be my sidekick judge, remember? I can't do this without you. Call me when you get this, okay? Love you."

Julia hung up but continued to stare at Jessie's contact picture on the screen. It hadn't been the first time recently she hadn't been able to get through to Jessie, who seemed to be flitting out of the house more and more with no explanation.

"No answer," Julia said to Barker when she returned to the kitchen. "Do you think something is going on with her? She's been acting odd lately."

"She has?" Barker licked his fingers after finishing the cupcake. "This is really yummy. You're onto another winner."

"You're missing a lot in your writing cave." She ruffled his hair as she walked past, ready to release the ginger and raspberry cupcakes from their metal baking tray. "Something doesn't feel right."

"She's a teenager. It's her job to make you worry."

Julia smiled over her shoulder, knowing Barker was right, but it didn't dispel the unease twisting her stomach. Despite Jessie only having been in Julia's life for two years, and only legally having been her daughter for even less time, Julia's maternal instincts had been growing stronger with each passing day. She could read Jessie like a book, and she knew her daughter was hiding something.

"I think I'll come and watch you judge," Barker said after letting out a long and deep yawn. "The fresh air might do me a world of good."

"You need to sleep." Julia transferred the

cupcakes onto a fresh tray and began drizzling them with cinnamon icing. "Your days of pulling all-nighters are long gone, Barker Brown."

"I'm still a spring chicken! Forty is the new twenty."

"Where did you read that?"

"A magazine."

"Well, tell that to your body."

"I'm fine." Barker stretched out and cracked his neck. "Another cup of coffee and I'll be as good as new. Besides, I don't want to miss my wife judging alongside *the* Tony Bridges."

"Something tells me you're more interested in seeing Tony Bridges."

"Nonsense." Barker appeared behind Julia and wrapped his hands around her waist, nuzzling his nose against her neck. "There could be a hundred Tony Bridges in a room, and I'd still only see you." His warm lips brushed against her skin, sending a tingle down her spine. "What time does the bake-off start, because I thought we could—"

Before Barker could propose his idea, a loud and frantic knocking echoed down the hallway from the front door. Barker continued kissing Julia's neck; as lovely as it felt, she couldn't ignore the door.

"That's probably Jessie." Julia pulled away when the knocking turned into banging. "How much do you want to bet she's forgotten her keys again? *Okay, okay! I'm coming!*"

Julia opened the door to the icy wonderland, but Jessie wasn't there to greet her. Instead, Julia's father, Brian South, stood on her doorstep as snow swirled around him, baby Vinnie clutched against his chest. He had three stuffed bags slung over his shoulder, and what appeared to be a travel cot crammed under his arm.

"*Dad?*" Julia ushered him inside when she noticed his wide-eyed panic. "Has something happened?"

"It's Katie." His voice trembled. "She's had an accident in Ibiza."

"An accident? When? Is she okay?"

"About an hour ago." He dropped the bags on the ground and leaned the cot against the hallway table. "Her friend was crying so much on the phone I could barely understand her. Something about a banana boat and a broken leg."

"Who's broken their leg?" Barker appeared in the hallway. "Hi, Brian."

"Katie," Julia answered, her hand drifting up to her mouth. "She only left for the airport yesterday."

"I should have listened to my gut!" Tears collected in the corners of her father's eyes. "I knew it was a bad idea for her to go on holiday with all her old modelling friends. They start acting like kids the second they're all together in a room. Add in the sun, and the all-you-can-drink bar and something like this was *bound* to happen." He inhaled deeply as Julia rested her hand on his shoulder. "I can't stay. I need to get to the airport. My flight leaves in two hours. I was lucky to find something in this weather."

"Is there anything I can do?" Julia asked. "Do you need me to drive you or—"

"Vinnie." He passed the baby over. "I can't take him with me. I'm going to be stuck in a hospital in the middle of Ibiza. It's no place for a baby. I'm sorry to ask, Julia, but I'm desperate."

"You want *me* to look after Vinnie?" Julia heard the panic in her voice as she struggled to hold up her surprisingly heavy fourteen-month-old baby brother. "For how long?"

"Until Katie can fly home again." Brian checked his watch before swooping in to kiss Vinnie on the cheek. "I really need to get on the road. The snow is going to slow me down. Everything he needs should be in his bags. You have my number if there's an emergency. You're a star."

Brian kissed Julia on the forehead, waved to Barker, and left as quickly as he had arrived, slamming the door behind him. With her wriggling brother in her arms, Julia turned to Barker, her confusion reflected in his blank expression.

"*Dada*?" Vinnie reached for the front door, his feet pushing against Julia with startling strength. "*Da-da*?"

"Dada's gone on a little holiday," Julia said, the wobble in her voice barely masked by her panicked smile, "but I'm sure he'll be back soon. It looks like you're going to be spending some time with your big sister. Doesn't that sound like fun?"

Vinnie looked up at Julia and then down the hallway at Barker; tears and wailing followed immediately.

2

"I knew I had one somewhere." Julia produced a pink car seat from the cupboard at the end of the hall. "Sue left it here for when I look after the twins, but I haven't needed to use it until now. Do you know how to fit one?"

"Do *I* know?" Barker replied as he held Vinnie at arm's length. "I thought *you'd* know."

"I've never done it before." Julia put the car seat on the hallway floor and stared at it as though waiting for it to reveal its secrets. "This seems like a thing a man would know how to do. It's sort of like flatpack furniture, right?"

"And since when have *I* been good at flatpack?" Barker knocked on the wonky and wobbly bookcase he'd attempted to assemble to house his collection of first-edition crime novels. "Call your sister and ask. She'll know how to do it."

"I'm not calling Sue to ask how to fit a car seat!" Julia cried. "It's embarrassing. How hard can it be?"

"Hard enough that we're having this conversation." Barker sighed. He handed Vinnie over to Julia and snatched up the bulky contraption. "It's a good thing that I love you. Let me see if I can figure it out."

Knowing Barker would rather try to fit a car seat in the snow than be left alone with Vinnie, Julia breathed a sigh of relief, glad to have escaped venturing into the cold for now. She let Vinnie down onto the floor and steered him into the sitting room, his tiny legs wobbling as he walked.

"Bah!" he called as he clung to the coffee table with both hands, his knees bending to punctuate his cries. "*Bah!*"

"Bah?" Julia echoed. "What is Bah?"

"*Bah!*" he cried, his face scrunching. "*Bah!*"

Panic flared in Julia's chest. She admired anyone who looked after children full-time, but at thirty-nine years old, it was something she'd never experienced. She'd babysat the twins for her sister, Sue, for a couple of hours here and there, but it was always a relief to hand them back when the time came. Staring into Vinnie's tiny eyes while he grew increasingly wound up repeating *"Bah! Bah! Bah!"* on a loop, she felt the walls and ceiling closing in around her.

How long would her father be in Ibiza with Katie?

One day?

Two days?

A week?

More?

"Breathe, Julia," she reminded herself. "He's a baby. How hard can it be?"

As though to show her, Vinnie swiped a half-full cup of lukewarm peppermint and liquorice tea onto the floor. It bypassed the hearthrug and bounced off the edge of the stone fireplace, shattering on contact. Tea and porcelain flew in all directions, triggering Vinnie's cries. Julia swooped in and scooped him up. He thrashed and wriggled against her like a contortionist.

"Bah! Bah! Bah! Bah! Bah!" he screamed as he fought her grip. "*Bah!*"

Barker hurried back in, snow-covered and shivering in his pyjamas. Julia was pleased to see he was without the car seat.

"Did you figure it out?" she asked as Vinnie grabbed fistfuls of her chocolatey curls.

Barker gave his phone a celebratory pat. "With a little help from the internet. Are you okay? He looks like he's trying to pull your hair out."

"I think he is."

"*Bah!*"

"What is Bah?" she cried as she untangled her hair from Vinnie's tiny fingers and strong grip. "Do you understand what he's saying?"

Barker tilted his head as Vinnie repeated his chant over and over, his plump face growing redder and redder with each syllable.

"He sounds like a sheep."

"A *sheep*?" Julia gritted her jaw. "Serious answers only, please!"

"No, he really does sound like a sheep." Barker unzipped one of the bulging bags to reveal a vast collection of stuffed toys. He dug around until he found a tatty woolly sheep. He squeezed its stomach, and it let out a crackly 'baaaaaahhh' noise from a concealed speaker.

"Bah?" Barker said as he waved the toy in front of Vinnie's face. "Is this what you want?"

Vinnie's eyes lit up as he snatched the toy from Barker, his whining and thrashing ceasing straightaway. Sensing that the beast had been tamed for the time being, Julia placed him on the sofa. As though his request had been a simple one, he played peacefully with the stuffed animal, squeezing its stomach repeatedly to let out its grainy call.

"You don't suppose my dad put an instruction manual in there, do you?" Julia stared longingly at the bags. "What have we got ourselves into?"

***

As it turned out, Brian had left some instructions, although sparse ones. In his rush to gather Vinnie's things, he had found time to scribble a rough schedule on the back of an empty envelope. The schedule began at 6:30am with 'wake up and milk', continuing through a variety of milk feeds, meals, and activities, leading up to 'bedtime with a book' at 6:30pm. Assuming Brian had given him his breakfast and first milk feed of the day, Julia picked up at 'lunch at 11:45am ... he'll eat ANYTHING.' Unsure of what 'anything' meant for a fourteen-month-old baby, she consulted the internet and discovered that a small bowl of soup with bread was a suitable meal.

Without the assistance of a baby highchair, Julia helped Vinnie work his way through his lunch on the kitchen counter, not that he needed much assistance. He dunked his bread with gusto, splashing it and smearing it on his face with an infectious grin.

With food in his belly, Vinnie seemed content to play with his plethora of farm-themed stuffed toys, each of them providing a different single syllable sound. A little after noon, he was ready for his 'two-hour nap. NO MORE, or he'll be a NIGHTMARE at bedtime.' The travel cot was surprisingly easy to set up next to Julia and Barker's bed, and Vinnie fell asleep the instant his head hit the pillow. Leaving Barker to nap on the bed alongside him, Julia sat in the corner of the bedroom and flicked through her mother's handwritten recipe book as the snow fell outside like icing sugar dusting a Victoria sponge.

Vinnie stirred at two, and Barker followed soon after. Julia gave Vinnie his third scheduled milk bottle of the day while Barker shaved and showered. With an hour to spare until the bake-off started, they packed Barker's car with the cupcakes and Vinnie's essentials and set off slowly down the winding lane.

"Your car would have struggled down here," Barker remarked for the second time, the fresh snow crunching under the tyres.

"My car would have been *absolutely* fine," Julia shot back, knowing she was more than a little defensive of her precious vintage, aqua blue Ford Anglia. "She's lived through her fair share of winters."

The journey, which generally took less than five minutes, took almost fifteen thanks to Barker taking the twists and turns of the lane at a pace so slow it would have been quicker to walk. When they emerged in the heart of the village, it took Julia a moment to notice the large tent that had been erected on the village green thanks to its white shell blending in with the snowy backdrop. Barker pulled up in the alley next to Julia's café, behind Jessie's yellow Mini Cooper.

"Well, she's around somewhere," Barker said as he turned off the engine. "Is she still not picking up her phone?"

"No, but she's sent me a text message." Julia showed Barker the 'BUSY!' message on her phone. "I think that's her way of saying she's alive, so please leave her alone."

Julia unstrapped Vinnie from his car seat. She had wrapped him up in a tiny green scarf with matching gloves and a hat. With her help, Vinnie hobbled across the green, his little boots leaving deep indents in the fresh snow. Barker hurried behind with the cupcakes.

"Ah, *Julia*!" Brendan, the competition organiser and head of the Cotswold Baking Society, greeted her with a beaming grin. "Aww, is this your little one? He looks *just* like you!"

"He's my brother," Julia explained. "It's a long story. This all looks great!"

She looked around the giant tent. It was surprisingly toasty thanks to large electric heaters in each corner. A laminate floor had been laid, with two rows of pink gingham-covered tables in the middle, no doubt for the entrants' cakes to sit and be judged by Julia and Tony. Seats lined the perimeter, and a tea and coffee station waited at the far end. Without needing to be told, Barker headed there with the cupcakes.

Julia thought Brendan Jones was an unlikely

head of a society, let alone a baking one. He was young, late-twenties at the latest, with boyish good looks and a style Jessie had described as being 'geek chic' when he had visited the café to offer Julia the role. He had a sweet smile with deep dimples and slickly styled, quaffed, dark blond hair, which added a couple of inches to his petite height.

"I can't thank you enough for doing this," Brendan said as he consulted a clipboard. "I've heard a lot of great things about your café, and I have to say, it didn't disappoint."

"I'm happy to do it! Is Tony here?"

"Not, yet," Brendan said with a flat smile that left Julia feeling cold. "Have you met him?"

Julia shook her head. "Have you?"

"Unfortunately. I apologise in advance."

"For what?"

"Anything he says."

Before Julia could ask Brendan to elaborate, he hurried off to stop a young worker unplugging one of the heaters. Barker finished unwrapping the cupcakes and re-joined her, keeping a safe distance from Vinnie, who was on the floor hitting his sheep against the laminate while letting out piercing squeals.

"What kind of judge are you going to be?" Barker asked. "I can see you being exactly like Simon Cowell. Hitting buzzers and crushing dreams with a razor-sharp tongue."

"Hardly." Julia chuckled. "I'll be fair and kind. If I can offer advice, I will, but I won't be mean. That's not the point of today. We're here for some light village fun."

The tent entrance peeled back, and the familiar face of Julia's gran, Dot South, popped through. When she spotted Julia, she hurried in, followed closely by her short and plump fiancé, Percy Cropper.

"Gran, Percy!" Julia cried, her eyes wide as she took in their outfits. "You look ... new clothes?"

"Do you like?" Dot spun on the spot.

Dot and Percy were both dressed head-to-toe in so much brown fur Julia could barely tell where one article ended, and another began. She detected gloves, a hat, and a neck-to-toe coat, but it was hard to be sure.

"You look like two bears," Barker said.

"Thank you, kind man," Percy said, seemingly taking the observation as a compliment. "I got an amazing deal for the full set. Don't we look dashing?"

Despite it having been over a month since Percy had got down on one knee on Christmas Day to propose to Dot, it still took Julia by surprise to see her gran as part of a couple, especially since she had been single for as long as Julia could remember. Even though it was taking a while to get used to, Julia couldn't have been happier for them. They were opposites in most ways, but they suited each other like two pieces of a jigsaw puzzle.

"You look warm." Julia forced a smile. "Is it real fur?"

"No, dear!" Percy chuckled as he adjusted his round red spectacles. "We're not *monsters*! Fake fur, but you'd *never* know. Just as good as the real thing. Have a feel!"

"I'm okay." Julia shook her head as Percy offered his furry arm. "I believe you."

"Stroke the man!" Dot cried, nodding at the fur as she massaged her own furry arms. "It's as soft as butter!"

Julia glanced at Barker before sighing and running her fingers gently along Percy's fur coat. She offered him a smile in lieu of knowing what the correct response should be.

"Have a feel, Barker." Percy jerked his arm away from Julia. "One hundred percent genuine imitation fur! It's all the rage."

"Where?" Barker delicately stroked Percy's arm. "On the streets of Russia?"

"We're entering a new ice age!" Dot announced, wagging her gloved finger. "It's in *all* the papers! Don't you kids read the news anymore? That's what's wrong with this generation. Didn't I say that, Percy?"

"You did, Dorothy."

"Illiteracy is still on the rise!" Dot cried. "I *predicted* this would happen!"

"You predicted it in December," Julia reminded her.

"I was a little off with the dates." Dot fluttered her eyelids. "*Small* details! You're all too busy with your telephones and computer programs to notice what's really going on, tipping and tapping away while the real world passes you by."

"And I suppose believing in a new ice age is the real world?" Barker muttered under his breath.

"I *heard* that!" Dot snapped.

"I meant you to."

"You'll see who's laughing when this snow is still here in July! You'll be *begging* to know where we got our furs, and, by then, the price will have *rocketed*, and we'll all be living like cavemen trading sticks and stones for *scraps* of meat! And do you know what I'll say when that day comes, Barker?"

"What?"

"I *told* you so!"

"Don't get too worked up, Dorothy." Percy looped his furry arm through hers. "Not at our age."

"Speak for yourself, dear." Dot craned her neck and looked around the tent. "I don't suppose Tony Bridges is here yet?"

"Not yet," Julia said. "Any particular reason?"

"Oh, no!" Dot let out an airy giggle. "I just wanted to say hello and tell him that I *love* his radio show."

"You do?" Percy frowned as he looked up at Dot. "I didn't know that about you, Dorothy."

"Well, I'm a complex woman, dear. There's much to uncover. I actually won one of his radio contests once. Do you remember, Julia? You, Sue, and I went to that strange castle spa in Scotland because of him."

"I'll have to make sure to thank him," Julia said sardonically, remembering that the trip to Scotland had resulted in Julia solving yet another murder.

"I see Vinnie is playing with Bah." Percy nodded at the child. "Precious little thing. Are you babysitting?"

"Sort of." Julia inhaled sharply. "Dad had to run off to Ibiza. Katie's broken her leg on a banana boat."

"Banana boat?" Percy squinted through his glasses. "What's that when it's at home?"

"Well, it's a boat," Barker explained.

"Mm-hmm?"

"And it's shaped like a banana."

"How *novel*!" Percy clapped his hands together. "Did you hear that, Dorothy? A boat in the shape of a banana. What will they think of next?"

"Yes, dear." Dot dismissed him with her hand. "You said Katie *broke* her leg? If that woman had two brain cells, she'd be dangerous! As it stands, she has just the one."

"*Gran!*"

"Well, you know what I mean." Dot tutted and rolled her eyes. "All that peroxide for her hair seeped into her brain, you see."

"Katie isn't so bad when you get to know her," Julia said, giving her gran a stern look. "She's actually really lovely."

"The dumb ones usually are, dear." Dot went to

push up her curls but stopped when she realised they were tucked into her giant fluffy hat. "They don't know any different."

"Aside from prophesying the end of days, insulting your daughter-in-law, and looking for Tony Bridges, was there something *else* you wanted, Gran?"

Dot's eyes lit up in the way they did whenever she had a scrap of fresh gossip to spread. "Percy and I just saw something rather *troubling* on Mulberry Lane."

"Troubling indeed," Percy echoed.

"Was it another sale on faux fur?" Barker asked.

Dot pursed her lips. "No, but I did see your Jessie heading up into the flat above the old flower shop with a man old enough to be her father!"

"Jessie?" Julia asked, stifling a laugh. "That doesn't sound right. Are you sure it was her?"

"My eyesight is as *sharp* as it's *ever* been!"

"I'm afraid I can't say the same for my own retinas," Percy jumped in, fiddling his glasses, "but I saw her too. It was definitely Jessie. Dark hair with bright red streaks?"

"That does sound like Jessie," Barker said, his tone taking a serious edge as he stepped forward.

"What did this man look like?"

"He was about your age," Dot started. "About your height, too. Less hair, and thicker around the middle. He was wearing a suit. He looked like the type of man who would get excited over iced buns and would break a sweat climbing a flight of stairs."

"Great observations, Dorothy." Percy patted her on the shoulder. "You're so perceptive."

"I know, dear."

Julia's feet froze to the spot at the confirmation that she had been right to assume something was going on with their daughter.

"I'm going over there," Barker said, his jaw gritting. "Whoever he is, I'll kill him."

"Barker, wait." Julia pulled him back. "There's probably an innocent explanation. Let's not jump to conclusions."

"Oh, I don't know, Julia." Dot lowered her voice and leaned in. "You hear all sorts in the paper these days. Young girls vanishing, never to be seen again. Who's to say she's not already in the back of a van being shipped off to Eastern Europe as we speak! I think you *should* be worried."

"Thanks, Gran."

"It's better to err on the side of caution." Dot

peeled back her thick gloves to check her watch on the inside of her wrist. "Where's that boyfriend of hers? Billy?"

"On holiday with his dad in Spain."

"And Alfie's gone to Birmingham to work on that hotel building job," Percy added. "Poor girl is probably shell-shocked from everyone leaving at once."

"C'mon, Percy." Dot yanked him towards the exit. "Let's be going. You still need to finish decorating your cake for the competition."

"Right you are, Dorothy!"

"You're entering the bake-off?" Julia asked.

"No, but Percy is." Dot puffed out her chest with a proud smile. "I didn't think it would be fair if *I* entered. You'd naturally want to give me top marks, and I didn't want to put you in that position. He's quite the baker, you know. He might be as good, if not *better* than you, Julia. He's a man of many talents."

"Well, if you're as good a baker as you are a magician, I look forward to judging your creation, Percy."

"You'll love it!" Percy clicked behind Julia's ear and produced a shiny fifty pence piece. Before she could be impressed by the trick, he dropped the coin, and half a dozen more rattled from his heavy sleeve. "Crumbs! Tatty bye!"

Dot and Percy ducked out of the tent arm-in-arm, leaving Julia and Barker in the silent aftermath of their bombshell. Barker's eagerness to march to Mulberry Lane to beat down the door of the flat above the florist was palpable, and she didn't blame him. A similar feeling rose in her chest, but one thought overrode everything else.

"We need to trust her," Julia said, clutching his hand. "She's a bright girl. There's probably an innocent explanation. You know what Dot and Percy are like. They're probably hallucinating from the suffocating heat of their fur."

Barker nodded, but Julia knew neither of them believed that. She might have questioned Dot's observation skills, but having Percy describe Jessie's very particular hair confirmed their accuracy.

"We need to trust her," Julia repeated, more for her own benefit. "She's never given us a reason not to."

Before either of them could dwell, the tent entrance ripped open again, and a tall man with silver hair and dark sunglasses marched in. A skinny and tall young man scurried behind, juggling an armful of bags, followed by a slender, glamorous, dark-haired woman in a thick fur coat, which certainly looked more genuine than Dot and Percy's. Evidently not having noticed the weather when she dressed that morning, the newcomer wore a leg-exposing pencil skirt and snow-covered heels.

"You must be Tony." Julia held out her hand to the man, who suited the descriptor of being a silver fox better than anyone Julia had ever met. "I'm Julia, it's so nice to meet—"

"Of course, I'm Tony," he snapped, ripping off his coat and tossing it over Julia's outstretched arm. "Who else would I be?" He yanked off his glasses and threw them over his shoulder, and the scrawny young man somehow dived to catch them. "Wow. Is this *it*? Hardly *The Great British Bake Off*, is it?" Tony's eyes snapped down on Julia, the icy blue of his irises more chilling than the snow. "You there, what did you say your name was? Julie?"

"Juli-*a*."

"Whatever." Tony sighed, as though bored with her voice already. "Get me a cinnamon latte would you, Julie? Almond milk, no sugar, and I want it exactly seventy-six degrees, no more and no less."

"I—"

"Don't talk to her like that!" Barker snapped, stepping in front of Julia. "Who do you think you are?"

"Tony Bridges," the man said with another sigh. "Award-winning radio disc jockey. And *you* are?"

"Her husband."

"Oh, excellent." Tony patted Barker on the shoulder. "Then you can help her with the latte. Seventy-six degrees."

Brendan hurried over and pried Barker and Tony apart with his clipboard.

"Tony, I see you've met your fellow judge, Julia South-Brown, owner of the quaint *Julia's Café* just across the green. You'll be working together today."

"Charmed." Tony shot Julia a split-second glance. "Listen, Branden, is it?"

"Brendan."

"Branden, we need to discuss my fee." Tony wrapped his arm around Brendan's shoulder and marched him off. "Crikey, what is that smell? Smells like gone-off soup!"

Tony dragged Brendan into the corner of the room, leaving Julia and Barker to linger awkwardly with the young man and the glamorous woman.

"I apologise for my husband," the woman said, a Spanish twang to her silky accent. "My precious Tony gets cranky when he skips lunch."

"*Cranky*?" Barker snapped, glaring in the direction of the DJ. "He's lucky I didn't knock his head off! Who does he think he is talking to people like that? He's nothing like he is on the radio!"

"My precious Tony works very hard," the woman explained with an unfazed smile, as though his outbursts were to be expected. "Wakes up very early for the radio show. He doesn't mean what he says. My name is Camila. It's so nice to meet you, Julie."

"It's Ju..." Camila walked off to join her husband before Julia could correct her.

The young man, who Julia assumed was Tony's unlucky assistant, dragged the bags over to the edge of the room. He popped out a foldable canvas chair and then a small table, on which he sat a glass with a bottle of sparkling water.

"Light village fun you said?" Barker muttered to Julia.

"There's never a dull moment in Peridale." Julia bundled Vinnie up. "I think I've detected the source of the 'gone-off soup' smell. C'mon, let's take him to the café to change. I have a cinnamon latte to make."

3

With the assistance of an internet tutorial on Barker's phone, they successfully changed Vinnie's nappy on the counter in the kitchen of Julia's café. Much to Barker's vocal dislike, Julia made Tony's latte to his exact specifications, justifying it by making lattes for everyone else in the tent too. She knew it would be a long shot, but she hoped the drink would act as a peace offering to make their afternoon smoother than their introduction.

"You don't get a second chance to make a first impression," Barker reminded her as they walked back to the tent with the lattes and Vinnie. "The man is a first class—"

"*Radio DJ*," Julia cut Barker off and nodded down at Vinnie. "Tiny ears have a *habit* of picking up *naughty* words. The last thing we want is for my father and Katie to return to a corrupted child."

The crew and Brendan were grateful for their lattes. Tony snatched up his cup without so much as a thank you, leaving two cups behind. Camila took one and smiled her thanks, leaving behind the last cup. Tony's young assistant eyed it up, but hung back, his hands clenched together. Sensing that he was scared to overstep an invisible boundary that Tony had put in place, Julia picked up the cup and walked over to him.

"I made them for everyone," Julia said with a soft smile. "Do you like lattes?"

The young man nodded, his eyes flitting to Tony, who was busy talking to his wife in hushed tones. Julia pushed the cup towards him, and after a moment of hesitation, he accepted it with a shaky smile.

"I'm Julia, by the way."

"Oliver," he replied, his voice delicate. "I'm Mr Bridges' assistant."

"You're not allowed to call him Tony?"

Oliver shook his head before taking a sip of the hot drink.

"Is he always like this, or have I caught him on a bad day?"

Oliver parted his lips to reply, but he stopped himself. His eyes flitted to Tony. Julia followed his gaze to see that the DJ was glaring at them.

"*Boy!*" he called, clicking his fingers. "I don't pay you to stand around chatting. Do your job and put those signs up."

Oliver thrust the latte back at Julia with an apologetic smile. He dropped down to one of the bags and produced a thick pile of paper along with a roll of tape. Julia watched as he flitted around the tent sticking bold 'NO PEANUTS ZONE' signs under the pink and blue bunting, ruining the quaint atmosphere Brendan and his team had spent all morning creating.

"It's like he takes pleasure in treating people like rubbish," Barker said to Julia, loud enough for Tony to hear if he was paying them any attention, which he wasn't. "If only people knew what he was really like. His radio ratings would plummet overnight."

"I'm here for the cakes, and that's it. I'm not going to let—"

The tent entrance ripped open, cutting off Julia mid-sentence. A redheaded woman dressed in an outfit more suited to horse-riding than baking stormed in. She scanned the tent, her eyes narrowing to slits when she landed on Tony, whose back was turned to them as he spoke with his wife. The redhead stormed past Julia, snatching the latte from her hand as she went. A waft of horse manure followed in her wake.

"*Oi*, Tony Bridges!" the woman roared, causing the DJ to spin around. "This is for Rocky!"

The feisty redhead tore the plastic lid off the paper cup before tossing its contents in Tony's face. Hot cinnamon latte splashed against his skin, soaking his hair and shirt. Steam rose from the liquid as he stumbled back with a throaty roar.

"Watch your back. Karma is coming for you." The woman spat on the ground, tossed the cup at him, and marched out of the tent, pushing past Julia and Barker on the way.

"*Tony*!" Camila cried, hurrying to her husband as he clawed at his face. "Oh, my precious Tony!"

"It's *burning*!"

"Seventy-six degrees to be precise," Barker muttered, holding back a laugh. "It's hardly volcanic, mate. Calm down."

"*Dammit, Oliver!*" Tony squinted through his pain at his assistant. "You *should* have *stopped* her! What's the point in you being here?"

Oliver, who was on the other side of the tent, turned bright red as he lingered with the leftover signs in his hand, clearly unsure if he should get closer.

"Tony, I'm so sorry!" Brendan rushed to the DJ's aid. "I have no idea what to say! Who was that woman?"

"How should *I* know?" Tony cried. "You'll be hearing from my lawyer first thing in the morning! Where's the bathroom?"

"W-we don't h-have one," Brendan stuttered.

"*What?*" Tony's eyes fully opened as his wife dabbed at his face with a tissue. "What do you expect—"

"You can use my café," Julia interjected, saving Brendan from Tony's wrath. "It's across the green. I'll take you now."

Tony batted Camila's hand away and stomped across the tent. Leaving Vinnie with Barker, Julia hurried behind, overtaking and leading the way to her café. After unlocking the door, Tony walked straight to the bathroom, knocking into chairs as he went. The door slammed and locked, leaving Julia to linger and listen to loudly muttered expletives and running water.

"Do you need anything?" Julia called through the wood after knocking. "I have ice or—"

"*Shut up*, woman!"

Julia surprised herself by making an unpleasant hand gesture at the door. Even though he couldn't see her, it made her feel better. She dropped her hand when the little bell signalled the café door opening. Oliver crept in with a fresh shirt on a hanger.

"It was supposed to be for later," Oliver whispered when he realised his boss wasn't there. "Is he—"

"I'll deal with this," Julia whispered back. "Go, before he takes it out on you again. I've dealt with men like Tony Bridges before. He doesn't scare me."

Oliver's eyes met Julia's, and he smiled. He couldn't have been much older than Jessie. Julia wondered how a young man with a disposition such as Oliver's could get himself employed by someone like Tony. Oliver draped the shirt over the back of a chair and hurried out when the bathroom lock rattled.

"A fresh shirt," Julia announced when Tony marched out of the bathroom. "It's a little creased, but it will do the job."

Tony's face was bright red, but she suspected that was more from embarrassment than actual burns. He snatched the shirt from her, and, instead of going back into the bathroom, began unbuttoning in front of her. His body was decent for a man in his early fifties. He had some muscle definition and a slightly protruding stomach that gave Julia the impression he ate out at fine restaurants every night but also attended the gym semi-regularly. His skin was thoroughly tanned, but it was the kind of artificial deep tan that only came from hours of lying on sunbeds in tanning salons. From the way he casually undressed in front of her to the way he treated people, Julia concluded he suffered from a toxic mixture of vanity and arrogance that resulted in a more inflated ego than she had ever encountered.

"Did you know that woman?" Julia asked as Tony shrugged on the fresh shirt.

"Why would I have known her?"

"She seemed to know you."

"Well, I didn't know *her*!" Tony's fingers fiddled with the buttons. "She's probably a crazy fan who didn't win one of my phone-in competitions. The world is full of nasty people."

Ignoring the irony of his statement, Julia turned to the tent while Tony tucked his shirt into his jeans. Wrapped-up villagers walked to the tent from every direction, all carrying cake boxes. Julia glanced at the clock on the wall; the bake-off started in ten minutes.

"I assume I'm going to be judging this alone?" Julia said without turning to him. "It's probably for the best."

"Excuse me?"

"The bake-off." Julia nodded in the direction of the tent. "It starts soon."

"*And*?"

"I just thought you wouldn't want to do it after threatening to sue Brendan."

"Oh, that wasn't a threat." Tony walked across the café and ripped open the door. "But that's for my lawyer to deal with tomorrow. Today, I have a job to do, and I'm nothing if not professional."

Without waiting for Julia, Tony made his way across the snowy green, fastening his cuffs. Julia locked her café and followed behind, smiling and nodding to the villagers who were turning up for their bakes to be judged. For their sake, she hoped Tony would honour his promise of being professional, but that hope immediately shattered when she heard more shouting coming from the tent.

"I'm not doing this with *her* here!" Tony cried, pointing at one of the women behind the gingham table. "I *refuse*! She's *stalking* me!"

Julia looked at the woman Tony was pointing at. She was standing behind a cake box, unwinding a multi-coloured scarf from around her neck. She appeared to be of a similar age to Tony, and was plump and short, with a sharp greying bob that looked like it might once have been blonde. Her eyes were beady and sunken behind her round, red cheeks, and her short nose pointed up at the tip. Julia's immediate judgment was that the woman bore an unfortunate resemblance to a pig, but she shook that thought away, feeling bad that her mind had gone there.

"Aren't you happy to see me, Tony?" the woman called as she pulled a red woolly hat from her head. "I baked your favourite."

The rest of the entrants awkwardly found places at the table, all observing the unfolding argument with shared confusion.

"Bev, *why* do you do this?" Camila cried. "Tony is with *me* now. You *need* to leave."

"I'm not going anywhere, darlin'," Bev announced as she fixed her greying bob in a compact mirror. "Believe it or not, I'm here to have my cake judged fairly. I'm not here for my ex-husband. You're more than *welcome* to him."

Tony grabbed Brendan and marched him off into the corner as Bev walked to the other side of the tent to lay her things on one of the chairs. The whispering started immediately; all eyes fixed on Bev, waiting for her next move. Julia turned to Tony and watched as he spat venom at Brendan through gritted teeth. The organiser leaned away, his clipboard pulled close to his chest. Sighing, Julia walked over and stood between them.

"You can't disqualify someone for being a judge's ex-wife," Julia said in her calmest voice. "It's not fair."

"*Fair*?" Tony yelled. "She's been making my life a *misery* since the day I left her! She's been following me. I've had to get the police involved. She's *one* crazy stunt away from getting herself slapped with a restraining order!"

"I—I—I—" Brendan stuttered. "If that's what

you—"

"No." Julia shook her head and pinched the bridge of her nose. "I don't know the woman, and I don't know you, Tony, but fair is fair. This is a small village baking competition. The outside world doesn't come into it. It's about cakes. That's it."

"*Cakes*?" Tony cried, jabbing his finger at Julia's face. "You little—"

"I don't care *who* you think you are, but I'm *not* falling in line." Julia batted his finger away, puffed out her chest, and planted her fists on her hips. "You're not the only judge here, and something tells me you're here for the money and don't know the first thing about baking."

"Are you going to let *her* talk to *me* like that?" Tony asked Brendan. "*I'm* the star attraction!"

"And *I'm* the one with the baking knowledge," Julia butted in, pushing her face in front of Tony's gaze. "There are a lot of people in this tent who have come to compete, and they've spent a lot of time baking those cakes, your ex-wife included. Now, are you going to behave yourself for the next two hours so we can get through this, or are you not the professional you claimed to be?"

Tony glared at Julia for what felt like an age, his icy eyes pinning her to the spot. Despite feeling uncomfortable and sensing that her face was as red as his, she held his gaze without blinking.

"Whatever," Tony muttered.

He pushed past Julia and marched over to his foldable chair. He snapped for Oliver to pour him a glass of sparkling water. Julia looked around and noticed that all eyes were on her. She assumed she'd been whispering, but from the shocked faces of the villagers, it was evident she'd spoken a little louder than she'd intended.

"Julia, I'm so sorry about him," Brendan said. "He has a bad reputation in industry circles, but there aren't many local Peridale celebrities to call on for things like this. I didn't expect him to be this bad! I've been doing these bake-offs all over the Cotswolds, and the other celebs have had their diva moments, but nothing on this scale. I don't even know why he agreed to come. He's been asking me to triple his fee all morning! Do you think he's really going to sue me for the coffee thing?"

"I wouldn't put it past him." Julia glanced at Tony as he slurped sparkling water and glared at the watching crowd.

"He must think I'm making a profit doing this." Brendan's voice took on a desperate tone. "Once

I've collected the entrant fees, paid for the tent, and paid the judges, there's nothing left. I do this because I love baking, and I want to spread that love to as many people as I can! If he sues me, I'll be ruined. Maybe I should call the whole thing off?"

"No, no." Julia shook her head as she looked around the tent. "Don't do that. Look how many people have put effort into baking for this. They came to be judged, and that's what we're going to do. If Tony wants to throw his weight around, that's his prerogative, but I'm not going to bow to it, and neither should you. In two hours, it'll all be over, and you'll never have to see him again."

"I'm in awe of you, Julia." Brendan's smile beamed. "How did you get so strong?"

"Let's just say there's a reason Barker is my *second* husband." Julia patted him on the shoulder. "Men like Tony are all bark, no bite. Like the coffee-slinger woman said, karma will get him eventually."

***

When the rest of the competitors had arrived with their cakes, Julia was glad to see that the ones who had overheard her altercation with Tony were in the minority. It also meant that a handful of people were going to miss out on her cupcakes thanks to her underestimation of the turnout, but at least most of them didn't know how awful Tony was—although she was sure they would by the end of the afternoon.

"I would like to welcome everyone to the first Peridale Bake Off!" Brendan announced, his voice magnified by a headset microphone. "The first of many, I hope! What a *wonderful* turnout! Did you all have fun baking your cakes for our judges?"

Half of the crowd cheered. The other half grumbled.

"I'm going to guess most of you already know Julia South-Brown?" Brendan motioned for Julia to join him, and, as earlier-directed, she stood on his right at the front of the tent. To her surprise, strong applause filled with cheers and whistles greeted her. "If you've been lucky enough to sample Julia's baking, you'll know why she is here, and if you haven't, I strongly suggest you make it your priority to visit her café as soon as you can. Are you ready to judge, Julia?"

"I am, Brendan," Julia said into her own headset microphone. Her voice echoed around the tent, bouncing back at her. "Oh, dear. Is that what I sound like?"

Laughter tittered through the watching crowd of familiar faces as Julia's cheeks burned. Barker caught her attention from the edge of the tent where he was sat trying to contain Vinnie; he gave her two big thumbs up.

"Of course, Julia can't judge this competition alone. Our next judge needs no introduction." Brendan paused as he gave Julia a knowing, sideways glance. "You know him best for his popular afternoon show on *Cotswold Classic Radio*, but today he's the second half of your judging panel. Put your hands together for Tony Bridges!"

Tony stepped forward and took his place on the other side of Brendan. To Julia's surprise, the applause and cheers for Tony were quieter and more unsure than the greeting she'd received. From the less than impressed faces in the crowd, it seemed the word of Tony's earlier outburst had already spread. Bev, the ex-wife, stood in the centre of the first table, fanning a yawn instead of clapping.

"Are you ready, Tony?" Brendan asked, his lack of enthusiasm breaking through his fake smile.

"I wouldn't want to be anywhere else," Tony said sarcastically. "Have you reminded everyone about my allergy?"

"Ah yes," Brendan said. "If you didn't read the flyer or haven't seen the two dozen signs around the tent, Tony is allergic to peanuts. I assume all of you have been kind enough not to include them in your cakes. If you have, I'm afraid you'll have to withdraw from the competition." Brendan waited for someone to come forward, but no one did. "Excellent. So, without further ado, let's get this bake-off underway! Good luck and may the best baker win!"

Beginning with the first table on the right-hand side meant Shilpa Patil, who worked in the post office next to Julia's café, was the first to be judged. She was dressed in a beautiful yellow sari, complementing her bake, which appeared to be a plate of biscuits served with ice cream.

"These are nankhatai," Shilpa explained proudly. "They're an Indian favourite, and I made them from my mother's own recipe. They can be sweet or savoury, but of course, I went for sweet today."

"How lovely," Julia said as she assessed the golden discs. "They look delightful. And the ice cream?"

"Mango kulfi." Shilpa produced two spoons

from behind the bowl. "I made it myself. I think it pairs wonderfully with the nankhatai."

"I thought this was supposed to be a cake competition?" Tony muttered under his breath, apparently not caring that his words were being amplified around the tent by his microphone. "Definitely no peanuts in this?"

"No." Shilpa shook her head, her cheeks reddening as she took a step back from her bake.

Julia picked up one of the nankhatai and scooped a small amount of the mango kulfi on top. She took a bite, making sure to smile at Shilpa as she did. The biscuit was sweet, reminding Julia of traditional Scottish shortbread. The mango kulfi was thick and refreshing, and Shilpa had been correct about it pairing nicely with the biscuit.

"I love it," Julia said after swallowing the mouthful. "You'll have to give me the recipe!"

"Tony?" Brendan prompted. "Thoughts?"

"It's a biscuit with ice cream," Tony mumbled through his mouthful. "It's nothing special."

Julia bit her tongue. The microphone stopped her from saying what she really wanted to. She smiled at Shilpa and nodded to let her know she'd done an excellent job.

Amy Clark was next up with her take on a

lemon cheesecake. Any hope Julia had of Tony being anything other than himself was immediately crushed. After a tiny bite of Amy's cheesecake, he spat it out into a napkin. Julia took a bite, and while it was a little on the sour side, it wasn't worth spitting.

"*Bloody hell*!" Tony cried after glugging from a water bottle. "How many lemons did you squeeze into that thing?"

"Three," Amy muttered, stepping back as she fiddled with her baby blue cardigan. "I thought it tasted nice."

"It does, Amy," Julia interjected before Tony could crush the poor woman any more. "You've done a great job, and you're on the right track, but maybe next time stick to a single lemon? It will make it *even* better."

Julia's compassion appeared to ease Amy's nerves. Julia pushed Tony toward the next cake before he could upset Amy any more than he already had. Unluckily for the villagers of Peridale, things weren't to get any better. He called Malcolm Johnson's floral-inspired sponge cake "disgusting", Roxy Carter's brownies "far too rich", and Evelyn Wood's cinnamon coffee cake "revolting"; Evelyn claimed to have "foreseen such comments" in her morning tea leaves. When they made their way to Bev's red velvet cake, Julia couldn't see how things could get much worse.

"I made your favourite, Tony," Bev said with a bite in her voice as she pushed the cake forward. "You always did like my red velvet cake."

"You're unbelievable, woman." Tony rolled his eyes as he dug his fork into a pre-cut slice. "I can't believe I was married to you for so long."

"The feeling is mutual, my dear." Bev folded her arms as she watched Tony lift the fork up to his mouth. "Try not to choke."

"I wouldn't be surprised if you'd poisoned the thing," Tony said before cramming the fork into his mouth. "I wouldn't put it past you."

"Don't flatter yourself."

Julia broke off a small piece of the cake and put it into her mouth. Her first impression was that the cake was light and fluffy and tasted of chocolate as it should, but she detected something different within the flavour. She recognised it, but she couldn't immediately put her finger on it. As she swallowed the cake, it came to her where she had tasted the flavour combination before. It reminded her of a chocolate bar Jessie had bought from an American import online shop. Jessie had loved it, but it'd been too sweet for Julia's tastes. When she remembered what the chocolate bar had been stuffed with, her heart skipped a beat as she turned to Tony.

Even if she hadn't remembered what the flavour was, it was evident from the red and clammy appearance of Tony's face what they had just consumed. He clung to the edge of the table and stared dead ahead at Bev. He tried to say something, but his breaths were shallow and strained.

"*Tony*?" Camila cried as she hurried over. "My precious Tony! What is wrong?"

"I think he's going into anaphylactic shock," Julia stated as she rested her hands on his shoulders. "There were peanuts in the cake. Where's his EpiPen?"

Camila stared at her husband, and then at Bev. Tears collected along her thick lash line.

"Camila, the EpiPen?" Julia cried. "There's no time for this!"

Camila nodded and hurried to the pile of bags at the front. She scrambled through her handbag while a deadly and suffocating silence dropped over the tent. Brendan hurried over with a chair for Tony to sit in. Julia attempted to steer Tony into the chair, but he stumbled back and missed the chair, landing with a thud on the ground.

"Call an ambulance," Julia said to Brendan. "Tell them to be quick. *Camila*? EpiPen?"

"I cannot *find* it!" she cried, panting through her tears. "It was in my bag this morning! It's *not* here!"

Julia dropped to Tony's side and attempted to open his mouth to allow air through. His skin was scorching to the touch, and splotchy hives were making their way up his swelling neck. He stared up at Julia, his gaze desperate as he suffocated on his own breath. It crossed her mind that this was the first genuine human emotion she had seen in those pale eyes all afternoon.

"Does someone know how to help him?" Julia called out. "*Anyone*?"

No one came forward from the shocked crowd. Julia looked back at Tony, but the wheezing had stopped; the life had drained from his eyes.

"I think he just died," Brendan whispered to Julia.

4

Despite no longer being a DI, Barker resurrected his former authority and ordered everyone to stay in the tent. The competitors all gathered near the tea and coffee station at the back, none of them daring to utter a word. Barker allowed Percy to leave to whisk Vinnie away to Dot's cottage across the green before the baby realised what was happening around him. Barker spent the unbearable minutes until the police and ambulance arrived attempting to revive Tony. Julia admired his resolve, but nothing could bring the man back.

Camila stood in the corner, staring at her husband, as Barker tried his best. She didn't cry or wail, she simply stood in stoic silence; Julia would have felt less uncomfortable if Camila had cried, if only to have filled the deafening silence with something other than Barker's frustrated pants.

Bev, the baker of the killer cake, remained behind her red velvet and stared at her dead ex-husband, mouth agape. Tears silently steamed from her unblinking eyes while her entire body remained as solid as a rock.

The assistant, Oliver, sat hunched in one of the chairs, staring at the ground, with his hands clasped against the side of his head; he was far too young to have witnessed such a thing.

It was almost a relief when Julia heard the sirens even though she knew it was too late. Two paramedics rushed in and took Barker's place. They attempted their work for ten minutes, but they pronounced Tony Bridges dead at 3:37pm. The announcement caused Camila to drop to the ground with a cry. The crowd gasped, and one of the paramedics rushed over. Oliver stood and began pacing like an animal in a cage, and the waiting crowd at the back broke their silence, their whispering anything but quiet.

"Once again, another death and Julia South just happens to be in the middle of it all," DI John Christie said, appearing behind Julia and making her jump.

"It's Julia South-*Brown* now."

"Ah, that's right. I wasn't invited to the wedding, was I?" DI Christie dropped his smug expression for a moment and looked seriously at Julia. "Let's cut to it. Barker says the woman whose cake killed the fella is his ex-wife?"

"That's correct."

"And they were all warned about his allergy?"

"Multiple times."

"And there's all these damn signs."

"Tony got his assistant to put those out." Julia glanced at Oliver, who was still pacing. "Poor kid."

"Poor Tony." DI Christie sucked air through his teeth. "Shame. My wife loves his radio show. She would have loved it if I'd got an autograph."

"More serious things are happening right now."

"I know. My wife's night is going to be ruined when I tell her he's been murdered. I'm the one who has to live with her."

Julia ignored his crass attempt at humour. "You're treating this as a murder already?"

"Scorned woman poisons allergic ex-husband with a peanut cake?" DI Christie leaned into Julia's ear. "I'd say it's a done deal. I'd appreciate it if you didn't muck up one of my cases for once, okay? Congrats on the wedding."

DI Christie muttered something into his radio before taking a step forward and clapping his hands together.

"Can everyone *settle down*!" Christie cried, pausing for the whispering to die down fully. "I know you've all been through a lot, but I'm shutting this site down and treating it as a crime scene. You're all going to be questioned one by one. Julia, can I use your café to hold them?" DI Christie turned to Julia, and she offered an unsure nod. "Excellent. You'll all follow one of my officers across the green to the café, and if I catch any of you running off, I'll personally see to it that the book is thrown at you. If you ask nicely, I'm sure Mrs South-Brown wouldn't mind sticking the kettle on while you all wait your turn. Now, which one of you is Bev? I'd like to speak to you myself."

Bev didn't look up from Tony, but all eyes shot to her, revealing her identity to the DI. He walked over and said something that made her eyes finally shift. The next thing he said made her shake her head and stumble back into the table behind her. Christie sighed and motioned for his officers to join him. When Bev realised what was happening, she tried to escape, but the officers were clever and had approached from either side of the table.

"*No!*" she screamed as the officers tried to calm her down. "No! I *didn't*! I *wouldn't*! I—I—You can't prove anything!"

"Cuff her, boys," Christie ordered. "We've got ourselves a wriggler."

Bev screamed her innocence as the officers dragged her out. Shortly afterwards, more officers turned up to lead the witnesses away and secure the tent. While they were being led out in a single-file line, Dot hurried over to Julia.

"If you get a chance dear, give Percy's cake a try. It really is very—"

"*Gran!*"

"Just a small bite won't—"

"Not the time."

"Righty-o, dear. I'll see you later!"

Julia gave the café keys to Barker. Instead of joining the line marching to her café, she moved toward Oliver, who had stopped pacing and was now staring into space. Julia rested her hands on his shoulders and directed him into one of the empty chairs at the edge of the tent. Julia gently rubbed his back, the way she did when Jessie wasn't feeling so well.

"It's okay to be in shock," she said quietly to him.

"Am I going to get in trouble?" He looked up at Julia with teary eyes.

"Why would you get in trouble?"

"Because I let Mr Bridges die." His voice cracked, and he dropped his head into his hands. "I should have done something to help."

"There was nothing you could have done." She continued to rub his back gently as he sobbed into his hands.

She stayed with Oliver until Christie snapped for her to join him by the red velvet cake. A forensics officer took photographs of it.

"I heard you tasted this, too?" he nodded at the two forks on the table. "Notice anything peculiar about the cake?"

"It tasted like a red velvet cake at first."

"And that's peculiar?"

"Because it didn't immediately taste of peanuts, which tells me they probably weren't baked into the cake."

"Do you think that's important?"

"It could be." Julia shook her head from side to side. "There were also no peanut chunks, so it was likely peanut oil."

"Peanut oil, but not baked into the sponge?" Christie arched a brow. "How can you be so sure?"

"Because, Detective, if enough peanut oil to kill a man had been baked into that cake, it wouldn't be standing up like it is now." Julia pointed her finger at the air bubbles in the light and fluffy sponge. "The oil was added after the cake was baked. Take my word for it, or don't."

"But why would she add it after?"

"Am I under arrest, Detective?"

"No."

"Then I assume I'm free to go. I'd like to make sure my café is being looked after."

Julia didn't wait for DI Christie to say otherwise. She lifted Oliver up, guiding him across the snowy green and into her café. She imagined that Christie was bad-mouthing her to every officer who would listen, but she didn't mind. She had helped Christie out enough times to know he must secretly respect her on some level.

Once Oliver was comfortable in a chair, Julia

grabbed her phone from her pocket and scrolled straight to Jessie's number. She pushed the phone to her ear and tapped her foot against the floor. For the first time that morning, Jessie picked up.

"Hello?" Jessie said.

"*Jessie*! Where are you?"

"Right here." Jessie's voice on the speaker merged with one right behind her.

Julia spun around. Jessie had just entered the café, her phone still to her ear. They both hung up at the same time. Julia's emotions at seeing her daughter ranged from angry to elated. She wanted to shout at her for ignoring her all morning, but she couldn't resist pulling her into a tight hug.

"What's happened?" Jessie asked as Julia squeezed her tight. "You're crushing my ribs!"

"I'm sorry." Julia let go and held her at arm's length. "A man died. *Where* have you been?"

"A man?" Jessie scrunched up her face. "Who?"

"Don't avoid my question."

"What question?"

"*Where* have you been?"

Jessie looked around the packed café as though wanting someone to help her.

"Nowhere." Jessie shrugged. "What's the big deal?"

"Where's nowhere?" Julia shook Jessie's shoulders. "Where have you been? You said you were going to help me with the bake-off."

"Just around."

"Around where specifically?"

"What's got into you, cake lady?" Jessie pulled her arms away from Julia and brushed the creases from her black denim jacket. "Since when have you wanted to keep tabs on me every second of the day? I'm eighteen!"

Julia felt the people close to them starting to notice something was going on. She inhaled deeply to calm herself, realising she was compounding witnessing a man dying with missing Jessie all morning.

"I'm sorry." Julia hugged Jessie again before kissing her on the forehead. "I was worried about you, that's all."

"Well, you don't need to worry." Jessie wiped the kiss from her head. "I'm fine. I need to go and call Billy. He'll never believe what he's missed."

It didn't take long for Johnny Watson, *The Peridale Post*'s editor and one of Julia's oldest friends, to turn up with his camera and notepad.

"I was supposed to cover the bake-off," Johnny said, fiddling with his glasses. "Sounds like I missed a lot! Me and Leah got stuck in the snow on the top road. What happened?"

"A man died from an anaphylactic shock thanks to a peanut-loaded red velvet."

"Is it true what they're saying?" Johnny whispered as he leaned in. "That it was *the* Tony Bridges?"

"Word really does travel fast around here."

"I think we're about to set a sales record for the paper." Johnny clicked his camera and took a picture of the packed café. He pulled out his notepad and flicked to a fresh page. "In your own words, what happened?"

"Johnny—"

"The people *deserve* to know!" Johnny jumped in with a cheeky smile. "C'mon, Julia! Help an old friend out. He's a celebrity! I promise I won't even cite you. You can be 'an eyewitness' and still get your story out there."

"You know me better than that, Johnny." She patted him on the arm as she shook her head. "Sorry."

Johnny slapped his pad shut and shrugged. "You can't blame a guy for trying, right? It was worth a shot."

Despite Julia's refusal to give him a story,

Johnny hung around, and it turned out she was the only one unwilling to spill the beans to the paper. The other witnesses practically fought each other to give Johnny their accounts of the tragedy. Julia tried to ignore the noise as she served people their promised free drinks, but the snippets she did hear were already wildly exaggerated.

"According to Amy, Bev said 'I've poisoned you, ha!' while Tony was 'waving his hands around and trying to strangle her'," Julia said to Barker, who was in the kitchen helping Jessie whip up some sandwiches to pass around. "I don't remember any of that happening, and I was stood right next to him."

"Don't worry, Christie will be able to tell the fact from the fiction," Barker assured her. "Half their statements will be useless, but he needs enough that match up to put together the timeline. The ones that don't fit in will be discounted."

"And yet I bet Johnny still prints them in the paper." Julia picked up a finished tray of sandwiches. "I wish I'd stayed at home and watched a film after all."

***

After everyone, including Julia and Barker, had given their witness statements, Julia locked the café and set off into the night towards Dot's cottage to collect Vinnie.

"We're looking after him?" Jessie cried as they added more footprints to the green. "For how long?"

"As long as it takes for Katie to be able to fly home."

"But babies cry."

"I know," Julia replied.

"And poo."

"We're aware," Barker jumped in.

"Why couldn't he stay at the manor?" Jessie frowned. "That crazy housekeeper could look after him."

"Hilary is probably looking after Katie's dad, who, if you recall, is very old and wheelchair-bound and needs a lot of care and attention. We could ask to swap if you really don't want to have a baby in the house?"

Jessie huffed and shook her head. "Whatever. But if he stops me sleeping, I'll—"

"Throw a tantrum?" Barker cut in. "Then we'll have *two* babies to look after. That's no way to talk about your uncle."

"*Uncle*?" Jessie cried.

"Technically," Julia said with a chuckle.

"But he's *one*!"

"Fourteen-months," Julia corrected her.

"That's the *same* thing!"

"Not according to Katie."

Even though Julia didn't resent having to look after her baby brother, she was relieved to find out that Dot had fed him his dinner and milk, and even more relieved to see him fast asleep on Dot's sofa after his bedtime bath.

"He's been as good as gold," Percy said as he passed Julia the sheep toy. "It's always a pleasure."

"Can't say his father was like that," Dot said as she pushed a hand through her curls. "Let's just say there's a reason I only had one child. Vinnie is a delight compared to Brian."

Barker headed back to bring his car around, leaving Julia to pick up Vinnie, who, thankfully, didn't stir from his deep sleep. After loading the car and fastening Vinnie into his car seat, they set off on the slow journey up the snowy lane to their cottage. Vinnie remained silent while Julia unfastened him, and he didn't even wake up when Jessie slammed her car door. The moment they stepped over the threshold, however, Vinnie woke up and exercised his lungs to prove it.

5

Julia couldn't bring herself to set a 6:30am alarm for the morning, but, as it turned out, she hadn't needed to. At 6:30am sharp, Vinnie woke up and rattled the side of his travel cot. Still half-asleep, Julia managed to snooze through her baby alarm clock for three minutes, but when the grace period was over, Vinnie tossed his head back and belted out his tearless cries.

Barker shot up in bed, panting as though waking from a bad dream. "What's going on?"

"Go back to sleep," Julia said, pulling Barker back down to his pillow. "It's Vinnie. We're looking after him, remember?"

"Oh, yeah." Barker relaxed back into his pillow, his eyes closing. "Do you want me to get up with him?"

Julia appreciated the offer, but she wasn't upset when Barker resumed his snoring. Knowing there was no sense in them both missing out on sleep, Julia pulled on her slippers and dressing gown before lifting Vinnie out of his cot. His head rested on her shoulder, and the crying stopped.

"You're getting heavy, big boy," Julia whispered as she carried him through her dark cottage and into the kitchen. "Aren't you glad Sue brought us her spare highchair last night?"

Julia slid Vinnie into the pink plastic chair before making him up a bottle of milk for his first feed of the day. While Vinnie drank his morning milk, Julia made herself a much-needed cup of peppermint and liquorice tea. Tony Bridges' death didn't cross her mind until the toast popped out of the toaster.

"Why would Bev want to kill Tony like that in front of so many people?" Julia mused to Vinnie as she munched through her wholegrain toast loaded with butter. "Do you think something's fishy too?"

Vinnie burped, and a milk bubble emerged from his nostrils. Julia couldn't help but laugh, and Vinnie joined in. She finished her toast and grabbed her phone from the counter. She was relieved to see a text message from their father, sent in the early hours of the morning.

"Dadda landed in Ibiza and found a hotel. Oh dear, he says mummy has fractured her leg in *two* different places and is waiting to go into surgery." Vinnie let out another giggle before resuming his milk. "Looks like we're going to be spending a lot of time together, kid."

After replying to her father and sending a picture of Vinnie to show that everything was going fine, Julia took him and her tea into the sitting room. She flicked through the channels until she landed on cartoons. Thankfully, Vinnie's attention was captured right away, leaving her to scribble in her notepad and sip her first tea of the day.

She flicked past her recipe for the lemon and Earl Grey cupcakes, which nobody had got to try, and started on a fresh page. In the middle, she wrote 'Tony Bridges' in a circle before writing everything she knew around his name. The first words she wrote were 'arrogant' and 'egomaniac', followed by 'well-advertised peanut allergy.' After filling that page with information on Tony, she flicked to the next page and headed it with 'CONNECTIONS!'

She wrote down 'Camila - the wife', 'Bev - the ex-wife', and 'Oliver - the assistant.' She almost put her pen down to stare at the notes, but she remembered another connection. 'Coffee-throwing lady - who is she???'

"What time is it?" Jessie croaked as she stumbled out of her bedroom, eyes half-closed and hair standing on end.

"Just past seven," Julia said after checking the clock on the mantlepiece. "Go back to bed. You can get another hour in."

"I'm up now." Jessie pushed on the bathroom door and locked it behind her. The sound of the shower started immediately.

Julia was anxious to talk to Jessie about what'd happened yesterday, but she knew the more she tried to push it, the more Jessie would push back. There was every possibility Dot and Percy had been mistaken, but Jessie wasn't acting like her usual self, and that scared Julia.

While Jessie was in the shower, Barker walked

into the sitting room in his underwear, scratching under his arm and yawning as wide as a hippo. After kissing Julia on the top of the head, he collapsed into the sofa next to Vinnie, who was too engrossed by a cartoon pig to notice anything going on around him.

"Do you want me to look after him while you're at work?" were Barker's first yawned words. "I don't mind."

"I appreciate the offer, but I think I'm going to stay home with him today. Jessie offered to run the café on her own. Mondays are usually quiet, and with the snow, I doubt many people will be venturing out, even if they are dying to gossip about what happened yesterday."

"Oh, yeah." Barker blinked hard after rubbing his eyes. "I'd forgotten about that. Are you going to be looking into it?"

"What gives you that idea?"

"Your notepad." Barker nodded at the pad she had unsuccessfully tried to push up her sleeve when she'd heard him coming. "You only use that when you're trying to suss something out or when you're writing recipes, and something tells me you aren't working on recipes at seven in the morning."

"I'm not looking into it," Julia said, which was

the truth, "but I'm also not *not* looking into it."

"Something feel off?"

"Hmm," Julia hummed through a mouthful of tea. "Can't you feel it?"

"I can." Barker stretched his arms above his head and let out another yawn. "It's too neat and wrapped up. Ex-wife kills ex-husband with peanuts in front of everyone and then denies doing it. If I'd gone to those lengths to kill my ex-wife publicly, I'd at least want to brag about it."

"Remind me never to divorce you." Julia tossed her pad onto the side table next to her tea. "I don't know. Let's see how things unravel. Perhaps Bev has already confessed everything."

"And if she hasn't?"

"Then we'll see." Julia shrugged. "What are you doing today?"

"Writing." Barker looked at the dining room door; his eyes filled with dread. "I lost all of yesterday. If I don't rewrite at least two scenes today, I'm toast. Speaking of which, is there any bread?"

"There's two for you, and two for Jessie," Julia said, kissing him on the hand as he passed. "Put some clothes on. You'll catch your death."

By 8am, Jessie was at the café to start the day's

baking, and Barker was shut in the dining room with a large mug of coffee and a stack of fresh paper to feed his typewriter. Vinnie devoured his breakfast cereal in what felt like minutes, and by 8:30am, he was down for his first hour-nap of the day.

Julia could have spent that hour doing anything she wanted, but with a sleeping baby and a frozen winter wonderland outside, she felt trapped in her cottage with only Vinnie's snores and Barker's rattling typewriter to keep her company. She sat on the couch and brushed Mowgli, reducing his fluffy Maine Coon fur by half while Vinnie's cartoons played in the background, not that she was focussing on the adventures of the tiny pink pig and her friends; her mind was fixed on Tony Bridges. It didn't take much to conjure up the look of fear she had seen in his eyes. He had known he was going to die.

"Do we have a dictionary?" Barker asked as he hurried into the sitting room, breaking Julia from her thoughts. "You looked miles away then."

"Dictionary?" Julia shook Tony to the back of her mind and tried to remember where she'd put it. "Under the armchair next to the window."

Barker lifted the chair and pulled out the giant

leather volume, which had been acting as a leg for the wonky chair for the best part of three years. Barker patted the book and smiled his thanks, leaving the chair slanted.

"What a boring day," she whispered to Mowgli.

When the morning's mail dropped onto the doormat just before 9am, she jumped up and ran to collect it, if only for something to do. She flicked through the stack of bills, but none of them interested her. Instead, she picked up that morning's edition of *The Peridale Post* and unfolded it to read Johnny's headline:

BODY AT THE BAKE-OFF! Beloved Radio DJ Dead, Age 52.

Johnny had picked a flattering photograph of Tony, showing him behind a microphone at the studio. Julia had always thought him good-looking, but that impression had faded after spending ten seconds in his company—not because he was any less handsome in real life, but because his personality had been ugly. She might have felt bad thinking ill of the dead, but as it were, she knew she wasn't the only one.

She took the paper through to the sitting room

and scanned through the story. It detailed Tony's early days living in Peridale before moving off to London to work for the BBC. He returned to the Cotswolds in his thirties to start his radio show—not that he moved back to Peridale, instead choosing a more modern home in the neighbouring village of Riverswick, where he lived with his wife, Camila. The story was filled with inflammatory quotes from 'eyewitnesses', most highly exaggerated. Julia's name was brought up a couple of times, once when being referred to as 'Tony's fellow judge', and later again when Johnny decided to add in 'Julia South-Brown refused to comment.' Julia smirked, knowing Johnny had likely got a kick out of his little dig.

She tossed the paper onto the coffee table after she was finished with it. Tony's terrible behaviour hadn't been mentioned in the article. Julia suspected Johnny was holding that back for next week's issue, to continue the story for as long as it sold papers.

Julia returned to the kitchen to refill her teacup, and when she spotted the dusty radio on top of the fridge, she pulled it down and tuned it to *Cotswold Classic Radio*.

"And of course, we're still talking about our

beloved Tony Bridges this morning," the male presenter said. "If you haven't already heard, Tony Bridges, presenter here on *Cotswold Classic Radio* for the past two decades, sadly passed away yesterday from a confirmed anaphylactic shock."

"They're saying it might have been murder," a female presenter added, "although I legally have to say *allegedly* on the end of that."

"Who would want to kill Tony?" said the man. "Coming up next, Bon Jovi's classic 'Living on a Prayer.' This one's for you, Tony. Hope you're listening, wherever you are."

Julia turned the radio off before the song started. Had she experienced Tony on a particularly bad day, or were the other presenters being professionals and saying what they knew the listeners wanted to hear? For a moment, she genuinely wondered if her experience had been a singular one, but remembering how fragile Oliver had been made by Tony's behaviour dismissed her misgivings. Oliver's demeanour wasn't that of someone experiencing their boss on a bad day, it was that of a boy who'd been systematically bullied by a man almost three times his age for a long time.

As Julia finished her second cup of tea, Vinnie

woke, and, to Julia's surprise, didn't do so crying. After changing him, Julia dressed him for the day and left him playing with his toys under the dining room table with Barker while she showered and dressed. After wriggling into jeans and a thick jumper, she tossed on a scarf and a coat and peeled back the bedroom curtains to look at the weather. The snow had stopped, and she could finally see patches of her green grass again, but it still looked bitterly cold.

"I'm going to take Vinnie into the village," Julia said as she coaxed her little brother out from under the table. "I think we both need the fresh air."

"Yeah," Barker said without looking up. "Okay."

"And then I'm going to ask around and see what I can find out about the case."

"No problem."

"And after that, I might take off all my clothes and streak around the village."

"Sounds good."

"Are you even listening to me, Barker?" Julia planted her hands on her hips. "What did I just say?"

Barker looked up guiltily, his fingers still

tapping on the keys.

"You look pretty," he said before looking back at the paper. "Have fun."

"C'mon, let's leave Barker to his work," she whispered to Vinnie as she closed the dining room door. "Maybe you'll grow up to be the first man who can successfully multi-task?"

Luckily for Julia, Sue had also dropped off a pram the night before. It was a bright pink one she had bought before finding out she was having twins, so it was still unused. Vinnie didn't mind the colour, and Julia quite liked how it complimented his tiny yellow winter coat.

They walked down the winding lane, the only tyre prints in the snow those of Barker's and Jessie's cars. The temperature was out of the minus figures, but it was still cold enough to keep the snow lingering around for the time being. They emerged into the heart of the village, and Julia was surprised to see the white tent had already been dismantled. The only hint something had even been there was the giant square of squashed grass on the green where the snow had melted. The rest of the grass was a mess of mushy snow mixed with mud thanks to all the pairs of feet that had trampled back and forth the previous day.

As Julia approached the café, she wasn't surprised to see that it was empty except for one customer sitting near the window. Julia pushed on the door with the end of the pram, the warmth hitting her immediately. Jessie looked up from a sheet of paper she was reading on the counter. When she noticed Julia, she stuffed the paper in her apron and stood up straight.

"What are you doing here?" Jessie asked, a brow arched. "It's dead."

"I needed to get out of the house." Julia unwound her scarf and started to unbundle Vinnie from his layers. "There's only so long I can stand listening to Barker drumming on that typewriter like he's angry at it. Has it been like this all morning?"

Jessie nodded. "She came in half an hour ago, and she's been staring out the window ever since. She hasn't even ordered anything. I thought about kicking her out, but she looks so upset."

Julia properly looked at the woman for the first time and realised who she was. She passed Jessie her scarf before walking around the counter to grab a large chocolate chip cookie from the display case. She put it on a plate before making a latte.

"Keep an eye on Vinnie." Julia pushed the pram

behind the counter. "It'll be time for his lunch in about half an hour. Make him a sandwich but remember to cut the pieces small."

"You want me to *feed* him?"

"Is that a problem?"

"What if he bites me?"

"He won't *bite* you!" Julia held back her laughter. "He's a baby."

"He *might!*" Jessie pouted as she eyed Vinnie suspiciously. "I saw my fair share of crazy babies in the children's homes."

"Well, this isn't one of them. You'll be fine. He practically feeds himself anyway, and I'm not leaving if you really need help."

Julia approached Camila slowly; the woman hadn't looked away from the patch of grass on the green. Julia set the plate and cup on the table quietly, not wanting to startle the newly made widow. Camila's eyes drifted blankly from the green to the items on the table, and then up at Julia. She squinted, as though she couldn't place the face.

"Julie," she said, her Spanish accent giving her name an 'h' sound at the beginning. "This is your café."

"May I sit?" Julia nodded at the chair, deciding not to correct her name.

Camila nodded. Even in grief, Camila was still strikingly beautiful. She had thick, bouncy brunette hair, big doe eyes with dark lashes, and plump red lips. Her skin had a sun-kissed olive tone to it, which looked more natural than her late husband's tangy glow. She was bare-faced, exposing the dark shadows under her eyes. Had the woman slept at all?

"I'm sorry for your loss," Julia offered. "I know that doesn't mean anything right now, but I mean it. You shouldn't have had to go through that."

"Thank you." Camila half-smiled before breaking off a small piece of the giant biscuit. "It doesn't feel real."

"That's normal. You'll get there."

Camila put the chunk in her mouth and chewed it awkwardly before taking a sip of her latte. "I'm sure it's as good as they say, but I'm afraid I can't taste much of anything right now. Is that normal too?"

"You're still in shock." Julia reached out and rested her hand on Camila's. "Take it one step at a time."

Camila smiled before sliding her hand away and resuming her gaze out the window. Julia had so many questions, but she didn't want to bombard the grief-stricken woman.

"I didn't know where else to go," Camila said. "Home didn't feel right without him. I think I was led here because this was the last place we were together. And now I am alone because of Bev. I should have listened to my husband when he said that woman would be the death of him."

"Did Tony really think that?"

Camila nodded. "She was obsessed. Would not leave him alone. They divorced two years ago, but she never let him go. I tried to make her leave before Tony got to the tent, but she would not even look at me. I am the woman who ruined her marriage, or so she thinks."

"Were they still together when you met Tony?"

Camila nodded again. She took a long sip of her latte before continuing. "I was Tony's assistant. We spent a lot of time together. He would tell me how awful his marriage to Bev was. He wanted to get out for years, but he was scared to leave her. He feared what she would do. It was only when we fell in love that he got the courage to leave, but it might have been easier if he'd stayed."

"What did Bev do?"

"What didn't she do?" Camila forced a dry laugh. "In the early days, she'd stand outside our house watching us. It was terrifying. We called the police so many times, but she always left before they got there. Then, she started posting notes through the letter-box in the middle of the night, threatening both of us. I was scared to go to sleep because I thought I'd wake up with her standing over me, holding a giant knife. It took her a year, but she stopped in the end. Neither of us had seen her until yesterday."

Tears collected in the corners of Camila's eyes, which Julia took as her cue to leave the woman alone with her latte and biscuit. She had given Julia a little to work with without being pushed too hard, and Julia wasn't about to start interrogating a grieving woman. She retreated to the kitchen where Jessie was attempting to feed Vinnie sandwiches, but his mouth was clamped tight, and he was tossing his head from side to side.

"He won't eat!" Jessie cried. "Why won't you eat?"

"Probably because you're trying to feed him like you'd feed Mowgli slices of ham." Julia took the sandwich from Jessie and placed it on the little shelf on the pram. It only took Vinnie a second to pick it up and cram it into his mouth. "See. Patience."

"When did you get so good at baby whispering?"

"You'd be surprised how quickly you pick it up."

"I'm fine not knowing." Jessie sighed. "I never want kids."

The revelation took Julia by surprise. They'd never talked about the possibility of Jessie wanting kids one day, but she hadn't expected a flat-out refusal.

"*Ever*?"

"Why would I?" Jessie arched a brow. "They're so annoying. Why would anyone want a baby?"

"Well, it's a little piece of you and another person." Julia watched Vinnie eat his sandwich; her heart swelled. "It's magic. You might change your mind one day. You're still young."

"And what about you?"

"I have you." Julia pulled Jessie in.

"But don't you want a baby that is part you and Barker?" Jessie wriggled away. "A little baker with an obsession for murder?"

"We haven't talked about it," Julia admitted. "We've only been married for five minutes."

"But is that what you want?"

"I—I don't know."

"You *must* know." Jessie rolled her eyes. "You've had all your life to think about if you want them or not. It's not rocket science."

Julia was slightly taken aback by Jessie's insistence that she answer. Julia had grown up expecting that she would one day have children. She had gone into her first marriage with Jerrad expecting that they would one day have children. Every time she brought it up, however, she was given a blanket 'we'll talk about it next year. The timing isn't right', and the timing remained 'not right' for all the twelve years they were married. As their marriage waned, Julia had given up the hope she would one day have a child. After their separation, and then their eventual divorce, she'd abandoned the idea altogether. Since then, to stem the disappointment, she hadn't allowed herself to think about it.

"Yes," Julia answered. "I would like to have a child with Barker one day, but we haven't discussed it yet, so don't go telling him that, okay?"

"Promise." Jessie held up her pinkie. "And for the record, Barker wouldn't say no. He loves you too much. He'd do anything for you."

Julia knew Jessie was right, but the old familiar phrase popped into her head.

"I don't think the timing is right," Julia said, her cheeks flushing as she watched Vinnie slap the tray in front of him like a drum. "Barker is really busy with his second book, and—"

"And then he'll be busy with his third book, and his fourth book, and then you'll be eighty-six and too old. Was the timing right when I broke into your café to steal cakes, and you made the crazy decision to foster a homeless girl?"

"Well, no."

"And was the timing right when Barker's cottage was destroyed, and he had to move in with us?"

"Not really."

"There's no such thing as the right time," Jessie said. "You just have to do things when you want to do them."

From the way Jessie's eyes glazed over, Julia sensed there was another meaning to what she was saying. Julia was about to push and ask what Jessie was up to, but the café bell interrupted them. Leaving Jessie with Vinnie, Julia pushed through the beads.

"Johnny Watson," Julia said with a warm smile. "Come to show off your new front page? Too late, I've already seen it."

"You like?"

"'Julia South-Brown refused to comment.'"

"I thought you'd like that." Johnny chuckled as he adjusted his glasses. "Actually, that's not why I came. I have some possible intel for you."

"Oh?" Julia pulled Johnny behind the counter, not wanting Camila to overhear. "Just keep your voice down, yeah? That's Tony's wife."

"Is it?" Johnny's eyes lit up. "Do you think she'll—"

"Want to give you an interview?" Julia jumped in. "Don't even think about it."

"Worth a shot." Johnny blushed as he ruffled a hand through his curly hair. "I was on the phone to my mum last night, and she brought up Tony Bridges before I did. Apparently, one of my cousins worked for him."

"Oh?"

"A kid called Oliver. I saw him here yesterday, and I knew I knew his face from somewhere. His mum is my mum's sister, and she's technically my auntie, but I've barely spent more than two minutes with her my whole life. None of them get on with her."

"I spoke to him yesterday," Julia whispered, glancing to make sure Camila wasn't eavesdropping. "What's the intel?"

"Well, that's it." Johnny shrugged. "My cousin was the assistant of Tony Bridges, who is now dead. What were you expecting?"

"Oh, I don't know. Something useful perhaps? What am I supposed to do with that?"

"I thought you might want to interview him? I assumed you'd be sleuthing?"

"You assumed wrong." Julia's phone vibrated in her pocket. She pulled it out; Barker had sent her a text message. "Hold on." She opened the message and read over it twice. "DI Christie has just texted Barker to tell him I *was* right about the peanut oil, and that it was drizzled over the slice we were going to eat. The rest of the cake was clean."

"What does that mean?" Johnny searched Julia's eyes with an excited smile.

"It means I'm sleuthing." Julia tucked her phone away. "It theoretically means that anyone in that tent could have contaminated the cake that killed Tony. Johnny, do you know where your cousin lives? He'll know more than most about Tony."

"Mum said something about the Fern Moore Estate."

"Flat number?"

"I don't know." Johnny scratched the side of his head. "Mum didn't mention it, but she might be able to find out. Like I said, we're just not that close to that side of the family."

"Find out for me."

"Keep me in the loop, okay?" Johnny asked. "If I give you Oliver, you have to tell me what you find out. Promise?"

"Okay, editor. I promise." Julia felt the familiar buzz of excitement in her stomach at the thought of chasing a lead. "Was there anything else?"

"Do you want to come to the pub for lunch?" Johnny hooked his thumb over his shoulder. "Roxy and Leah are there now. They asked me to ask you."

"I can't." Julia sighed as she peered through the beaded curtains at Jessie who was on her phone ignoring Vinnie in his pram. "I'm looking after my brother and, quite frankly, I don't trust Jessie to keep her eye on him."

"Bring him with you. We can discuss the case over a pub lunch."

Julia almost refused the offer point-blank, but then a wild thought crossed her mind. If Vinnie were her baby, would she put her life on hold forever, or would she try to incorporate him into her own routine as much as she could? There were, after all, worse places in the world for a baby than a quiet and warm village pub on a Monday afternoon.

"Okay, count me in."

Johnny beamed and turned to leave, saying he'd meet her there. As he walked to the door, Julia noticed that Camila had gone, leaving behind the cookie and the untouched latte. Julia had no idea if Bev was innocent or guilty, but she now felt a duty to discover the truth either way. Julia might not have liked Tony, but she had watched him die, and at least one person on the planet loved him, and she deserved the truth.

6

The pub lunch with her friends was just what Julia had needed. Leah and Roxy had fawned over Vinnie, keeping him occupied for most of the afternoon. Julia forwent her usual glass of white wine with her lunch for an orange juice, but it felt like a fair compromise.

Vinnie spent the rest of the day as well behaved as a fourteen-month-old could be. When Brian rang that evening to inform her that Katie had gone into surgery, Julia found she didn't feel dread in her stomach when he said he wasn't sure when they could fly home, as it all depended on how the operation went. Julia told him to take as long as they needed.

On Tuesday, Julia took Vinnie into the café and worked alongside Jessie. Thanks to most of the snow melting and no more falling, the residents of Peridale were more eager to venture out, and the full café meant there were always enough eyes on Vinnie in between his scheduled naps and meals. On Tuesday night, news travelled around the village that Bev had been released from the station without being charged thanks to 'insufficient evidence', and despite Julia's best efforts, DI Christie refused to hand over her home address because Julia had no useful information to trade.

"I bet you're still hiding something," he'd said. "You always are."

Although it'd been a fair comment, Julia really didn't have anything. Even though Vinnie was behaving, it was hard to chase information when no clues were falling into her lap.

She spent most of Wednesday trying to contact Johnny to see if he'd found Oliver's address, but he hadn't been able to get hold of his mother because he was too busy chasing stories for the paper.

With no way of contacting anyone involved in Tony's life, Julia almost resigned herself to considering the case a lost cause. She awoke on Thursday ready to let it go until something more substantial came her way. She sent Jessie to work alone and stayed home with Vinnie, which she did contently until the afternoon boredom set in after Vinnie's lunch.

"There's a soft play area five miles away," Julia called into the dining room. "I'm searching for 'fun things for babies to do.' Fancy an afternoon trip out?"

As it happened, Julia's distraction came at a moment when Barker desperately needed a break from his revisions. His editor had sent through a fresh burst of heavy edits, and she could sense he was losing the will to continue with each letter he pounded into the typewriter.

The soft play area was situated on a quiet, tree-lined road outside the village. It was next door to a petrol station, pushed back from the road by a large, and mostly empty, car park. Julia and Barker gave each other sceptical glances when they pulled into one of the empty spaces. If it weren't for the giant yellow 'Little Tots Treasures' sign featuring a monkey dressed as a pirate eating a banana, Julia would have assumed the sat nav had given them the wrong directions.

"It looks like a DIY shop," Barker muttered under his breath as he shut off the car's engine. "Are you sure this place is safe?"

"It had amazing online reviews," Julia replied, just as uncertainly. "Let's have a look inside. We've come this far. We can always leave."

Thankfully, the inside looked exactly as Julia had expected. It was colourful and airy, and apart from the exposed industrial ceiling, it bore little resemblance to its stark outer shell. A giant climbing maze with slides and ball pits took up most of the space, with a smaller area more suitable for children Vinnie's age at the far end. The sound of children's laughter echoed around the expansive space, only slightly softened by distant pop music playing from hidden speakers.

"Is this what parents enjoy?" Barker whispered to Julia.

"I don't think this is for the parents," Julia replied. "Although, I think I read that there's a coffee shop in here somewhere."

After paying for Vinnie's entry, they carried him to the toddler play area next to the promised coffee shop, where all the other parents were hauled up. A couple of them smiled and acknowledged Julia and Barker, but most silently sipped coffee, scrolling endlessly through their phones while their kids played to their hearts' content.

"Grab us some drinks," Barker said as he led a very excited Vinnie into the toddler area. "I'll watch him."

Vinnie broke free of Barker's hand and ran straight for the shallow ball pit where the other toddlers were playing. Julia retrieved her purse from her handbag and walked to the coffee shop counter, joining the line of three other women.

"You have a good one there," the woman next to her said, nodding at Barker as he sat by the ball pit with Vinnie. "I could only convince my husband to come here if they started serving beer and playing the football on a TV. Is that your first?"

Instead of correcting the woman, Julia found herself nodding instead. It was easier to pretend Vinnie was her son than explaining that her father's wife was also their age.

"I'm on my fourth." The woman pulled back her jacket to reveal a petite, but firm bump. "Let's just say it was a nice little surprise when I turned forty-two. I thought my days of changing nappies and doing midnight feeds were long behind me, but I guess I get to experience it all over again. Are you thinking of having any more?"

"Who knows," Julia said, unable to look the kind stranger fully in the eye. "I think so."

"Don't wait too long." The woman pushed on the bottom of her back, her face twisting. "It's true when they say it gets harder the older you get. I barely felt any different when I had my first in my twenties, but this feels like I have a fully grown adult living inside me. And the morning sickness! Don't get me started on that. I laughed it off when my midwife called me a 'geriatric mother', but geriatric sums up how this baby is making me feel."

They shuffled down the line, and the woman ordered herself a cup of decaf coffee and a large chocolate muffin. While the young girl made up her order, the woman turned and watched Barker play with Vinnie.

"You really did marry one of the good ones," she said. "He actually looks like he's enjoying himself."

The woman paid for her order and gave Julia a final smile before retreating to her table, where she resumed looking through her phone while she took large bites out of her muffin. Julia looked around the large space, and even though she hadn't noticed at first, Barker was the only man in there.

"I do have a good one," Julia whispered as she turned to the young server.

"Sorry?" the girl grumbled. "Actually, can you wait a minute? I was supposed to go on my break five minutes ago. Let me go see where Beverly is."

The girl pushed through a staff door, leaving Julia to stare at the cakes in the display case. They were almost certainly store-bought, probably delivered in plastic wrappers that morning, but she'd skipped lunch, and the double-chocolate muffin was calling her.

"Sorry about that," an older and deeper voice said; a hint of cigarette smoke wafted on her breath. "Kids these days are so impatient, aren't they? What can I get you?"

Julia's eyes met the new server's, and they recognised each other during the same split second.

"Bev," Julia said, her throat drying. "Hi."

"Hello." Bev's spine stiffened, and her smile slid off her face. "You were the other judge at the bake-off, weren't you?"

Julia nodded.

"What are you doing here?" Bev snapped.

"I've brought my baby brother to play." Julia hooked her thumb over her shoulder. "I didn't know you worked here."

Bev seemed to relax at hearing that Julia hadn't come specifically to see her, although her sunken, beady eyes remained unblinking.

"How are you doing?" Julia asked.

"You mean after I had to watch my ex-husband die and then be accused of murdering him?" Bev's voice was flat and cold. "I've never been better."

Julia scrambled for something to say to the woman whom everyone thought had taken advantage of her ex-husband's peanut allergy to kill him. Though she had been ready to let the mystery go, now that she had access to one of the key players, the investigative fire within her had the spark it needed to burn bright.

Before Julia could launch into the dozens of questions she wanted to ask Bev, another woman joined the line behind her. Not wanting to be directly overheard, Julia ordered two cups of coffee with two double-chocolate muffins. She paid and took them to the table closest to the toddler play area and waited for Barker to join her. When he did, he was red-faced and panting, but he seemed to be enjoying himself just as much as Vinnie.

"He has so much energy," Barker said as he collapsed into the chair next to Julia. He sipped his coffee. "I'm jealous."

"Do you remember Tony's ex-wife?" Julia whispered to Barker. "The one who baked the killer red velvet?"

"The pig lady?"

"Don't call her *that*!"

"So, you're telling me you didn't think that when you saw her?" Barker gave her a playful smile.

"That's not the point." Julia pouted before drinking her coffee. "Don't look now, but by some weird twist of fate, she works here."

"*Where*?" Barker craned his neck and looked directly at Bev. "Oh yeah, she does."

"What part of 'don't look now' didn't make sense to you?" Julia sank in her chair, embarrassed by her husband's lack of subtlety. "I'm surprised she's back at work so soon."

"Well, for what it's worth, I don't think she'll be a free woman for much longer. Christie couldn't charge her because the evidence is purely circumstantial and it would never hold up in court, but he's hellbent on cracking the case."

"And he's already decided that Bev's guilty?"

"It *was* her cake."

"You agreed that something felt off."

"And it still does," Barker said before taking a bite of his muffin, "but you have to look at what Christie's working with. No one is admitting to adding oil to that cake. He interviewed every single person who was in that tent, and he has nothing. His only lead is Bev, and he won't stop until he can prove that she did it."

As Julia watched Vinnie play, she felt increasingly more uncomfortable with DI Christie's investigative style. He was too stubborn and hot-headed to consider all the possibilities. If he thought something was true, he would mould an entire case around his assumptions, regardless of the evidence. Julia wasn't surprised she'd beaten him to the punch on so many cases since his ascendance to Barker's former position. When Barker had been Peridale's detective inspector, it had been a meeting of minds, even if Barker had tried to keep Julia at a professional distance. With Christie, she constantly butted heads. Unless Julia had useful information to trade, Christie didn't care what she thought, even if she ended up being right in the end. Of course, she was an ordinary woman who ran a café in a small village, and she had no right sticking her nose into official police business, but even she could see that she had a natural knack for unravelling mysteries, and that bothered men like Christie.

"Penny for your thoughts?" Barker nudged Julia's arm. "You've barely touched your muffin."

Julia tore off a piece and tossed it into her mouth. It looked moist, but it was stodgy and dry; she could have baked better blindfolded, standing on one leg in the middle of a power cut.

"What time does this place close?" Julia asked after forcing the mouthful down.

"Five." Barker checked his watch. "So, in two hours. Why?"

"Do you think it would look odd if we hung around until closing?"

"A little. You're going to talk to Bev, aren't you?"

"I just want to hear her side of things." Julia circled her finger around the top of the coffee cup's plastic lid. "Besides, Vinnie is having the time of his life."

Agatha Frost

7

An announcement at ten minutes to five asked parents to collect their children and head for the exit before the soft play area closed. Tears and tantrums broke out all over the building, and Vinnie was one of those noisy children. It took all of Julia and Barker's combined strength to get him out of the ball pit and back in his warm outdoor clothes.

After successfully wrangling Vinnie, Julia

carried him outside. The sun had almost set, and light flakes of snow tried their best to stick to the ground but melted on impact.

"Go home without me," Julia said as she passed Vinnie to Barker. "There's a cottage pie I made this morning in the fridge. Warm it up in the oven for half an hour, but make sure to let it cool down a little before giving it to Vinnie."

"How are you going to get home?"

"I'll call a taxi." Julia pulled her pink peacoat tight and buttoned it up. "We can't both stay here if we want to keep Vinnie in his routine."

Barker obviously didn't like the thought of leaving Julia, but she knew he would. He pursed his lips before letting out a reluctant sigh.

"Be safe."

"I always am." Julia kissed Barker and pinched Vinnie's cheek. "Go on, I'll be fine. I'll be home before you know it."

One by one, the other parents wrestled their unruly children into their cars, leaving Julia standing outside the entrance alone. She peeked through the window and watched as the staff members cleaned up the area after a long day of children running around the place.

Twenty minutes later, the lights turned off,

and, one by one, the staff members left, all bundled up in warm coats and scarves. When Bev emerged with another woman, Julia sank into the shadow of the large warehouse.

"Fancy a quick one at the pub, Pat?" Bev asked the similarly aged woman locking the doors. "It's been a while since we caught up."

"Not tonight, Bev," Pat said as she unlocked a panel on the wall with another key. "Another time."

Pat punched in some numbers on a keypad and stepped back. Metal shutters slid down, concealing the door for the evening. Without giving Bev a farewell, Pat tucked the keys away and headed to the last car. She climbed inside and sped off as though wanting to get away before Bev could speak to her again.

Still stuck to the side of the building, Julia observed Bev as she reached into her pocket for something. She had expected Bev to leave work alone, which meant that she'd been silently watching in the shadows for far too long. If she spoke now, Bev would be too freaked out to answer any of Julia's questions.

Not daring to breathe, Julia watched Bev pull a cigarette from a packet. She pushed it between her thin lips and attempted to light it, but the lighter sparked and fizzled.

"*Dammit!*" Bev tossed the lighter onto the ground after running her finger along the flint several times. "Just my luck!"

Bev yanked the cigarette from her mouth and forced it back into the carton. She pushed her hands into her pockets and set off across the car park in a diagonal line.

"What's the difference between sleuthing and stalking?" Julia whispered as she carefully followed behind, being careful to keep a safe distance.

Julia's heart stopped when her phone beeped in her pocket. She froze to the spot and scrambled for an explanation as she waited for Bev to turn around. However, luck was on Julia's side. Bev didn't turn around to bust her, and instead of vanishing into the night, she walked onto the brightly lit forecourt of the petrol station. Julia followed and lingered by the cash machine while Bev walked inside.

Unaware that she was being watched, Bev procured a shopping basket and began scanning the aisles. She grabbed a frozen microwave toad-in-the-hole, a bottle of red wine, two bars of fruit and nut chocolate, a box of cat food pouches, a fresh packet of cigarettes, and two lighters. While watching Bev count her coins from a tatty old purse, Julia considered her options. She could walk into the shop and pretend to bump into Bev, or she could continue following her until it felt like the right time to approach. Neither option felt ideal, leaving Julia to look around the petrol station for inspiration.

Julia spotted Pat filling her car, seemingly unaware that Bev was inside. Pat hadn't offered to give Bev a lift home, and Julia hadn't seen any other cars, which meant Bev was either walking to wherever she lived, or she was catching a bus from the dimly lit shelter across the road.

Not wanting to waste any time, Julia hurried across the forecourt and crossed the quiet road. She leaned against the bench in the bus shelter and steadied her breath so it didn't look like she had just run there. From where she was, she could watch the petrol station perfectly. If Bev left and didn't head to the bus stop, Julia could at least see where she was going and come up with another plan then.

While she waited for Bev to leave the petrol station, Julia retrieved her phone to see what had caused it to beep. It was a picture message from Barker. She clicked on the photograph to load it, and while it did, she looked up to check on Bev. She had left the petrol station and was walking slowly under the bright lights in Julia's direction. Pat, who had just finished pumping her petrol, spotted Bev but didn't try to catch her attention.

The moment of truth came when Bev reached the pavement. She lingered on the corner under a streetlamp and reached into her handbag for her purse. After a quick rummage, she pulled out what Julia knew was a bus ticket. Concealing her pleased smile at being right, Julia looked down at her phone, but her smile sprang free when she saw the picture Barker had sent to her. It was a selfie with Vinnie, who was grinning at the camera. Julia forgot all about what she was there doing and let the joy of the moment warm her through.

Julia only tore her eyes away from the screen when she sensed Bev had sat down next to her. Not wanting to seem too eager, Julia replied to the message before putting her phone away. Out the corner of her eye, she watched Bev finally light her cigarette. A sense of calm appeared to wash over her as she sank onto the bench. Without saying a word, she offered the packet to Julia.

"No, thank you. I don't smoke."

"Good choice." Bev sucked hard on the cigarette. "I gave up for twenty years. I only started again this week. I didn't even realise I'd bought the things until I was unwrapping them at home. Can you blame me after the week I've had? I'll give up tomorrow."

Julia decided against mentioning that she had witnessed Bev buying a new packet of twenty only minutes ago. For whatever reason, Bev wasn't questioning Julia's presence at the bus stop, and that was enough for her.

"Where's your husband and kid gone?" Bev asked after finishing her cigarette and blowing out the last of the smoke.

"Home."

"Separated already?" Bev tossed the cigarette stub onto the ground and crushed it under her shoe.

"Oh, no. We've only been married since Christmas. And the baby is my brother, Vinnie. I'm looking after him at the moment."

"Congrats on the wedding." Bev's voice lacked any of the sincerity Julia was used to. "Your brother is a baby? Don't tell me, your dad ditched your mum and married someone half his age?"

"Something like that," Julia replied. "Although, my mother died when I was a girl. But you're right about him marrying someone younger. Katie. She's the exact same age as I am."

"Isn't that awkward?"

"It was at first." Julia nodded. "It took nearly five years for me to get used to the idea, but, strangely enough, we're as close to a big happy family as you could get now."

"Lucky for some." Bev forced a bitter laugh. "Can't say I had the same experience. Well, not that it matters now that my ex-husband is dead and everyone thinks I killed him. If my luck carries on like it has, I'll be banged up behind bars before the end of next week. Evidence or not, they're going to fit me up for it, I can feel it. When I watched the police rip my house apart for a second time, all I could think was that, wherever he is, Tony would be finding all this hilarious."

"Did they find anything?" Julia asked, the cold chill in the wind forcing her to pull her coat tighter around her.

"There's nothing *to* find," Bev replied with a bite. "If I'd done it, they would have found something by now. It's been four days. It doesn't take that long to figure out if they've got something real. It would only take a single drop of peanut oil in my kitchen to charge me, but they won't find anything unless they decide to stitch me up. I didn't even have a bag of nuts in the cupboard. After two decades married to someone with a severe allergy, you get into the habit of not buying certain things."

Julia wasn't sure if she should believe her, but she found that she wanted to. She liked to think she was a good judge of character, and she didn't feel like Bev was lying to her.

"I was married for twelve years before I met Barker," Julia started, wanting to keep the conversation rolling. "I know what it feels like to be left for a younger woman."

"What was your replacement like?"

"Blonde, late-twenties, tall, thin." Julia allowed herself to smile while saying it; four years of distance since the end of her first marriage was enough to see the humour. "I came home from a long shift working in a cake factory to find all my possessions crammed into four black bags. He changed the locks and wrote me a formal letter to inform me he'd been having an affair with his receptionist and that he wanted to marry her."

"Bloody hell." Bev sucked the cool night air

through her teeth. "And I thought I had it bad. How did you manage not to kill him?"

"I wanted to," Julia admitted with a chuckle. "I'd given him what I thought were supposed to be the best years of my life, but when I came back to Peridale, I realised he'd done me a favour. It took me a while to rebuild my life, but it was for the best."

"You were still young," Bev said quietly. "It's not so easy to start again in your fifties with no money." She paused and pulled out a fresh cigarette. "I knew he'd been having an affair with Camila for a while. Years, in fact, but I looked the other way. They weren't exactly subtle. I was upset, broken even, but I wasn't surprised. What's that old saying? You lose them how you get them. I wasn't Tony's first wife."

"You weren't?"

Bev shook her head as she lit the second cigarette. She glanced at an approaching bus but stepped back into the shelter and let it pass by.

"Judy Bridges," Bev mumbled out the corner of her mouth as she balanced the cigarette between her lips. "They met during Tony's years working for the BBC. He was a news presenter covering the tiny stories nobody else would, and Judy was one of the weather girls."

"I think I remember her." Julia ventured into her memories from her teenage years. "Jet black hair?"

"It wasn't natural." Bev let smoke trickle through her nostrils. "She was mousy, but mousy doesn't get you noticed on TV. She wasn't a huge celebrity, but she was known enough. People seemed to like her from what they saw on the TV, but she was nothing like that. She was a cold, cruel woman. She wouldn't have spit on you if you were on fire unless you had something to offer her. They married six months after meeting. I think Tony was only about twenty-five then. They became the darlings of the news. Judy stopped doing the weather, and they somehow became anchors for the lunchtime news. People loved them, but Tony said it was all for show. They put on that act for nearly a full decade until they were replaced by less demanding people in 1997. They had a reputation for being trouble behind the scenes. Tony said they'd have blazing rows until the moment they went live and had to smile and pretend to be in love. When they were let go, no other channel would touch them. They were blacklisted from ever working in television again.

When *Cotswold Classic Radio* offered Tony a show back here, he didn't have much choice but to take it. By the end of 1997, Tony and Judy were living in a swanky flat in Cheltenham and Tony was commuting to the studio in Riverswick where they record the radio show."

Another bus approached, but Bev didn't move, so neither did Julia.

"How did you meet Tony?" Julia prompted.

"I was working as a cleaner at the studio," Bev continued after finishing her second cigarette. "He didn't look twice at me. Why would he? Even in my thirties, I wasn't a looker. I'd been single for years, and I didn't expect that to change. I certainly didn't expect that to change with *the* Tony Bridges!"

"But it did."

"Maybe my life would have worked out differently if I'd just left him alone." Bev stuffed her hands into her pockets. "I was cleaning the studio before Tony's show one day in the spring of 1998. He came in, and he was talking on the phone about needing an assistant. I was good at typing, and I had a good memory, so I volunteered myself. I thought he'd laugh at me, but he didn't. He just said 'okay, you're hired', and that was that. Judy would come in every so often, but Tony said she spent most of her time at home, spending his money on the TV shopping channels. She couldn't get work, and she didn't seem to want to. She was happy sponging off Tony while he worked at the station. I became his confidante, maybe even his only true friend." Bev allowed herself a flicker of a smile. "I never expected anything to happen between us, but it did. When he told me he loved me, I knew it was real. He had a beautiful wife at home, but he wanted to be with me. People used to call me Miss Piggy because of my nose, but he never did. He was sweet."

"*Sweet*?" Julia asked without realising.

"Back then, yes. He really was." Bev paused and looked out into the road as another bus came along. This time, she stood and held out her hand. "This is my bus."

"Mine, too."

The empty bus pulled up, and the doors shuddered open. Bev climbed on and flashed her return ticket at the driver. Julia followed, realising she had no idea where the bus was going.

"Do you go to Peridale?" Julia asked, quiet enough so Bev couldn't hear from her seat halfway up the bus.

"Furthest I can take you that way is the Fern

Moore estate," the driver said.

Julia considered telling Bev she had got on the wrong bus, but would she have another opportunity to speak to Tony's ex-wife, especially when she was being so candid?

"That's perfect," Julia said as she pulled her purse out of her bag. "How much?"

"£4.90."

"Wow." Julia almost gagged as she pulled out a fresh five-pound note. "I don't quite remember the busses being that expensive."

The driver's expression didn't crack as he snatched the note from her. He pushed a button on a coin dispensing machine, and a silver ten pence piece fell out. Julia scooped it up. The doors closed behind her, and the bus set off. She fell forward, catching herself on the pole. Bev had positioned herself halfway up the bus, on a pair of seats slightly raised thanks to a step. Instead of sitting on the outside seat, she was next to the window. Julia took that as an invitation to sit down, and Bev didn't tell her to move when she did.

"You were saying Tony used to be sweet?" Julia prompted, eager to continue her covert interview. "When did he change?"

"Judy fell pregnant in early 2000," Bev

continued, her gaze fixed on the windows as the dark countryside flashed by. "By then, Tony and I had been having our affair for two years. He didn't say he was leaving Judy, and I didn't ask him to. I never thought I'd be the woman he ended up with. I appreciated the affection and attention. Sad, really, don't you think?"

Julia smiled sympathetically, not wanting to let Bev know there were other ways to get affection than from a married man.

"I think Tony really wanted to be a father," Bev said with a soft smile. "He seemed excited when he told me. He told me he loved me, but he wanted to make his marriage work for the sake of the baby. I understood. How could I not? The baby deserved better than that. It deserved better than Judy being its mother."

"It?"

"Poor thing didn't make it far enough for them to find out." Bev's face tightened, and her beady eyes turned to slits. "Judy was a heavy drinker, and that positive pregnancy test didn't stop her. She was a train wreck. She cared more about wallowing in the ashes of her failed television career than her marriage. That was the death knell for them. She packed her things and left, and he didn't go looking for her. He came to me. The thing I never thought was going to happen actually happened. Their divorce was quick. I think each wanted out as much as the other, and there wasn't much to fight over. Judy had drained the accounts with her reckless spending, and Tony was living month to month from the radio station. By the end of 2000, Tony and I were married and living together."

The bus pulled up to another stop, and four tracksuit-clad teenagers climbed on. They each flashed their tickets and ran to the back of the bus. They were playing loud rap music from one of their phones before the doors had closed. The driver glared through the large rear-view mirror, but he didn't say anything.

"It was good at first," Bev continued, talking slightly louder thanks to the thudding music. "For a few years, actually. Tony's radio show was a hit. They were always giving him bonuses and upping his salary, but wasn't that the way back then? The recession hit, and that's when things really changed. They stripped everyone's salaries right back to the wire. Most of the DJs left, but Tony knew he didn't have many options. He had a hit show on a regional station, but that didn't mean the bigger stations would pick him up, especially with his name still tarnished with a lot of the higher-ups."

"How did the recession change him?"

"Tony is a very materialistic man. I mean, he *was* a materialistic man." A sad smile overspread Bev's face, and Julia thought she might cry. "The debt piled up, and the worse things got with the money, the worse Tony got. He was always trying some stunt or scheme to make extra money."

"Stunts?"

"Slipping in puddles in the supermarket for compensation." Bev rolled her eyes. "Nonsense like that. Rarely worked. The most he'd get was a small settlement to make him go away."

"And you were still his assistant?"

"No." Bev shook her head. "He couldn't afford me, and I wasn't going to work for free. I got a part-time cleaning job for a small law firm. It was pocket money, really. It wasn't really enough to help us out, it just meant a little extra for the food shopping every week. Two years before he left me, things started looking up for Tony. He was nominated for a national broadcasting award. He didn't win, but he was the first runner-up, which was enough leverage to ask for a pay rise. He threatened to leave, and they knew he would take the listeners with him wherever he went. He had offers off the back of almost winning that award, but I don't think he had the energy to start again."

The bus stopped again, and another group of teens hopped on. They flashed their tickets, and then, like the others, went straight to the back of the bus. The two groups appeared to know each other and quickly merged. Julia suddenly became very aware of where the gang might be getting off the bus.

"When did Camila come onto the scene?" Julia asked.

The bus stopped once again, and this time, Bev stood.

"This is my stop," she said, nodding for Julia to move out the way. "Thanks for listening to me witter on. Tony always did say I could chew the ear off anyone who would listen. See you around."

Julia stood and let Bev off. She almost followed, if only not to be left on a bus with a gang of teens, but she looked out the window, and in the darkness, she was completely disorientated. She considered moving up to the front of the bus until her stop but decided to sit back down in the same seat so as not to draw attention.

She watched Bev walk past the bus with her head down. She turned a corner and vanished from view as the bus set off again. It took Julia a minute to realise they were in Riverswick, but by then it was too late. Julia clasped her hands in her lap and looked straight ahead as the noise from behind grew louder. Swearwords, music, and laughter rattled her eardrums. She sensed that some of the kids had sat in the seats directly behind her. They were looking at her, that she was sure of, but she forced her neck to stay firmly stuck in the forward position.

The familiar concrete tower blocks of the Fern Moore estate came into view, and, as Julia had guessed, the gang jumped up and ran to the bottom of the bus before it came to a halt on the edge of the dimly lit courtyard. The teens burst out when the doors opened.

"C'mon, love," the driver called down the bus, staring at Julia in the rear-view mirror. "Are you getting off, or what?"

"I'll get off at the next stop," Julia said as she scrambled for her purse. "I'll pay for an extra ticket."

"End of the line." The driver pressed something on his control panel, and the main lights turned off, leaving only the floor lights and his cab light. "I haven't got all night. My wife's already got the bubble and squeak on the hob."

Julia wasn't sure her legs had ever moved so reluctantly before. She clung to each pole as she worked her way to the door, unsure if she'd be able to stand without their help. When she reached the open doors, she glanced back at the driver, but he simply nodded for her to leave.

Fern Moore, while technically sharing a postcode with Peridale, was a million miles away from the village. The two tall, U-shaped towers had been built in the early 1980s as cheap and dense council housing. In all those years, it had never shaken its reputation as being a hotspot for trouble. Peridale residents gave the estate a wide birth, and, for the most part, the Fern Moore inhabitants stayed away from the village. Julia had ventured into the estate on a handful of occasions, but it had yet to disprove its reputation.

The doors snapped shut behind her, and the bus drove off, leaving her alone at the bus stop. The streetlamp ahead flickered as more sleet fell. Julia looked over her shoulder, and even though she couldn't see much through the graffiti-covered plastic windows of the shelter, it sounded like the gang hadn't hung around.

Julia considered her options. Her first instinct was to call for a taxi, but after a quick rummage through her purse, she realised she didn't have enough to get her all the way home thanks to the extortionate bus fare. Her second instinct was to call Barker to ask him to have the money ready on the other side, but that would mean admitting to Barker that she was alone in the dark at the estate. Another option came to her in the shape of a yellow Mini Cooper and knowing that the driver of that Mini would keep a secret if Julia asked her to.

She pulled out her phone to call Jessie, but a preview of a text message from Johnny Watson was on her lock screen:

Spoke to my mum and I found out where...

Unable to resist the lure of information, Julia opened the text message, deciding she would call Jessie after finding out where Johnny's cousin, Oliver, lived. She was, after all, already at the estate.

Spoke to my mum and I found out where Oliver lives. Flat 88. Took ages for her to find out. He's always moving around. Remember ur promise, Julia! I want 2 know everything you find out from him. Good luck, detective!!!1! xx

Julia locked her phone. Without the bright screen to distract her from the flickering light, she realised the light had been blocked; she was sitting in the shadow of a gang of hooded and masked teenagers.

"Oi, Snow White," said one of the teenagers, his voice muffled by a skull balaclava. "Gimme your phone."

8

Clutching her mobile phone in her fist, Julia stared at the disguised teenager. His deep voice felt somewhat forced, and he had acne on the exposed section of his forehead. Sixteen? Seventeen at a push? Julia knew that should make him less scary, and it might have done if he were alone, but, having the backup of the other nine she quickly counted, his age meant nothing. Besides, a Fern Moore sixteen wasn't the same as a Peridale sixteen.

"Are you deaf?" the teen cried. "*Phone!*"

"N-no," Julia said, regretting the stutter. "No."

"So, you're not deaf?"

"No," she repeated firmer. "And no, I'm not giving you my phone."

A moment of dead silence followed before the gang erupted into a fit of laughter. They tossed their heads, slapping each other on the backs while Julia calculated her odds of pushing through and outrunning them all the way back to Peridale.

"Wrong answer," another of the boys said. "Don't make him ask twice."

Julia's fingers tightened around the phone. She attempted to swallow her fear, but the lump in her throat felt like one of Mowgli's fur balls.

"My husband is on the way," Julia lied. "He's a police officer."

"I'm shaking in my trainers." The skull teen reached into his pocket and pulled out a small black object. A click of his finger made a shiny blade appear, and even though there was no light, the knife still glittered in the darkness. "Now, are you going to give me your phone?"

Julia handed it over without a second thought. The phone lost all value as she stared at the silver blade. She doubted they would use it for the sake of a budget model smartphone, but she wasn't about to push them anymore to find out.

"And your bag," he prodded the knife at Julia's small handbag. "*Now!*"

Julia's fingers trembled as she pulled her bag off her shoulder. Her purse had little in the way of money in it, and her cards would be useless the second she was able to cancel them. The leader snatched the bag off her, and he tossed it to one of the lads at the end of the line, who ripped it open and dug through it.

"It's full of crap!" he cried, emptying the contents onto the floor.

He kicked through the items, but there was nothing of value, unless a gang of teenage boys needed a packet of tissues, a tube of cherry lip balm, half a packet of chewing gum, a small bottle of hand cream, an even smaller bottle of hand sanitiser, a handful of screwed up receipts, and Julia's notepad for scribbling recipe ideas and sleuthing notes.

"Check the purse." He pointed the knife at the end of the line. "She must have something. She's clearly from Peridale."

"£5.65 in change," the teen said as he tossed the coins onto the ground at Julia's feet, making her jump. "She has plastic. Three of them."

"PIN numbers." He pointed the knife at Julia. "And don't you dare think about lying to me."

"1979 for the blue one," Julia said quickly, her voice barely above a whisper. "3423 for the black one. 2456 for the other one. That's my credit card. I think that's expired."

"I didn't ask for your life story!" he cried, shaking the knife at her. "Did someone write those down?"

"Got it," another of the boys said as he tapped on his phone. "Wait, what was the second one?"

Julia scrambled around in her brain for the made-up number she had just given them.

"3423," she repeated.

Her pause seemed to go unnoticed, but she had a feeling they weren't over with her yet. The knife-wielding teen was practically licking his lips at the pearl engagement ring and gold wedding band on her left hand. She tried to hide them under her other hand, but she knew it was too late.

"Thanks for being so cooperative," the teen said with a smirk in his voice. "We'll just take your jewellery, and then we'll be on our way."

Julia clutched her hand and shook her head. The thought of giving up her mother's engagement ring and the wedding ring she had only worn for a month hurt more than the thought of being stabbed for them.

"Please," Julia said. "Please, leave me alone."

Tears clouded her vision. She knew she must have looked pathetic, but she didn't care. They had stripped her of her dignity, and she knew they were going to strip her of her rings too, and she couldn't do anything to stop them. When she felt gloved fingers tugging the rings off her hand, she didn't put up a fight. A hand ripped open her coat and snatched off the locket Jessie had given her exactly a year ago to celebrate their first anniversary of being in each other's lives. With their loot in hand, they vanished as quickly as they had arrived, scurrying off into the night, no doubt to try the cards in the nearest cash machine.

She didn't have time to mourn, she had to get away from the bus shelter as quickly as possible before they came back when they discovered she had been fast on her feet lying about all three of her PIN numbers. She scooped up the contents of her bag as well as much of the leftover change she could find.

With £2.40 clutched in her fist and her handbag slung over her shoulder, she ran across the estate to a phone box, one of the few that seemed to have survived the national cull. It stank of urine and was graffitied to within an inch of its life, but the soothing hum of a dial tone greeted her when she picked up the heavy receiver.

Staring at the '60p minimum' sign on the telephone, she reached for her phone to calculate how many calls she would be able to make. It took her searching both pockets to remember where her phone was. Clenching her eyes, she worked out the sum in her head.

"Four," she whispered to herself. "Four calls."

The first number she dialled was her own cottage. Eyes closed, she pressed the phone against her face and waited for Barker's comforting voice to fill her ears. Instead, she was greeted by a dead hum. Wondering if she'd dialled the number wrong, Julia hung up and waited for her 60p to be returned to her; the machine clinked and swallowed her money.

"*Seriously*?" Julia slapped the side of the machine. "I didn't get through!"

Julia slotted in more coins and almost dialled the number again until she realised that Barker had changed their number after their first attempt at a wedding had gone horribly wrong and people wouldn't stop calling them to offer their sympathies. Her fingers hovered over the numbers, but she had no idea what the new six digits were.

"Three ... Two ... Something," she said aloud. "Three ... Two ... *Six*?"

Julia suddenly flashed back to Barker handing her a scrap of paper and telling her to memorise their new landline number. She had said she would, but instead, she had added it to her mobile phone's contact list and left it at that. She never liked to admit she was one of those people who relied on technology, but being without her phone for the past ten minutes had left her feeling utterly useless.

After taking a second to peek outside to make sure the gang weren't already returning, Julia looked at the keypad again and tried to recall any other numbers she had committed to memory. She could only recall three, and none of them mobile numbers. The local doctor's, a number that hadn't changed since she was a little girl; her café's; and Dot's. Considering the local doctor's surgery and her café would be closed, Julia dialled her only option.

Much to her relief, the phone rang this time. She clenched the phone with both hands and mentally pleaded for Dot to pick up. The seconds dragged out like hours, and when the dial tone finally ended, and Dot's answering machine kicked in, Julia felt like she had been waiting all night. She considered leaving a message, but she knew there wasn't much Dot could do to help her if she did; her gran barely knew how to listen to her messages in the first place.

With only £1.20 left in twenty pence pieces, Julia had hit a wall. With Dot not answering, she had two options; risk calling Dot again in hopes she picked up this time, or risk calling the café on the off-chance Jessie was still cleaning after the long day.

"C'mon, Jessie," Julia whispered as she slotted in more coins. "I need you right now."

She dialled and waited, but like Dot's, the phone rang and rang and rang until it couldn't ring anymore. She imagined her dark café, all locked up, the rattling phone on the kitchen wall disturbing the peace. She looked down at her last bits of change. Back when she was a kid, it would have been enough to jump on the next bus heading to Peridale, but she doubted it would get her to the end of the street.

Feeling defeated, Julia threw her last coins into

the machine and punched in Dot's number again; no one answered. She listened to Dot's answer machine message with her forehead resting against the grimy telephone.

"Gran, it's Julia," she started, unsure of what to say to help her in this situation. "If by some miracle you figure out that you have a message, I need your help. I'm guessing it's around a quarter to six on Thursday night, in case you're listening to this next Tuesday. I'm in Fern Moore. I—I was mugged. They took my phone, and I have no money. Except for walking home, I'm pretty stranded. Can you believe it? I—I don't even know why I'm saying any of this. You're never going to hear it. If you are listening, try to get in touch with—" The line died, and the machine swallowed her last coins. "—Barker."

Leaving the phone box behind, Julia ventured into the heavier-falling sleet; some of it was sticking. She thought about walking to the next bus stop in hopes a driver would take pity on her, but after her last encounter, she doubted that would happen. Resigning herself to the long and wet walk home, Julia stuffed her hands into her pockets and set off. She only took two steps before she heard the familiar deep laughter of teenage boys.

Without taking a second to think, Julia dived behind the phone box and glued herself to it. She stopped breathing and listened as they walked right by.

"I can't believe she lied to you, Mark," one said. "Stupid Peridale Princess!"

"If I see her again, I'll finish her off," the one she presumed was Mark said. "I should have done it there and then."

Julia looked right ahead at the stairwell, and for the first time since stepping off the bus, she saw a glimmer of light at the end of the tunnel when she read the flat numbers spray painted on the wall.

"Flats 68-88," she whispered aloud. "*Flat 88*!"

The mugging had left her so shaken, she'd forgotten all about the text message she'd received from Johnny right before they took her phone. Not wanting to linger too long to find out what would happen if Mark and his pocket knife found Julia hiding behind a phone box, she followed the spray-painted arrow up the stairs to the third floor.

Her heart fluttered so much at the thought of finding the sweet and sensitive Oliver behind one of the doors, she didn't pause to consider what would happen if Johnny had given her the wrong number, or, even worse, if she had remembered incorrectly.

Pushing those thoughts to the back of her mind, Julia stopped when she reached the flat. It stood out from the other flats in more than one way. Whereas the others were stark and messy, 88 radiated a level of pride that was nowhere else to be seen along the exposed corridor. The door, which was behind a decorative metal gate, was painted baby pink. The window frame matched, and a flower box hung under crisp, white net curtains. The flower box was empty thanks to the weather, but she could tell bulbs had been planted and that something was in the early stages of sprouting.

It looked like a nice flat, but it didn't look like the flat that belonged to a quiet young man. Julia stole a glance over the edge of the walkway. The gang had taken root in the abandoned play park in the middle of the courtyard. Either way, her chances of sneaking away unseen had just halved. Even in the sleet, her pink coat and yellow jumper would stand out.

Now that she was truly out of choices, Julia wriggled her fist through the metal gate and knocked on the pink door. If Oliver lived there, she had a reason to be there, and if he didn't, she hoped whoever had taken the time to plant bulbs in such a bleak place would be kind enough to help a stranger who was wearing a coat the same colour as their woodwork.

"H-Hello?" a meek voice called through the door when it opened on the chain. "Who is it?"

"Hello there," Julia said, smiling when she realised she was speaking to an old lady who wouldn't look out of place on the streets of Peridale. "My name is Julia South-Brown. I think I may have the wrong flat, but I was wondering if you could help me. I appear to have found myself in a spot of trouble."

The door closed, and Julia's heart sank to the pit of her stomach. She was about to knock again, but the chain rattled, and the door opened. In full view, the lady was exactly the type Julia would have imagined painting her door pink and planting bulbs regardless of where she lived. She wore a white nightie that hit the floor thanks to her barely clearing five feet in height. She seemed nervous about the stranger knocking on her door, but her nerves seemed to ease when her pale eyes gave Julia the once over.

"Just a moment, please."

To Julia's surprise, the woman shut the door

again. The only hope Julia had to cling onto was that she didn't hear the chain rattle back into place. When the door opened again, the lady wore a thin green cardigan over her nightie.

"Just had to pop my teeth in," she said with a toothy smile. "You'll understand when you get to my age. Now, who did you say you were looking for, dear, and what's this spot of trouble you've found yourself in?"

"I was mugged," Julia explained. "They took my phone, my cards, and my rings."

The woman nodded with a sympathetic smile, although she didn't seem surprised or shocked by what she'd just heard. Julia wondered how many years one had to live in Fern Moore before growing numb to its ways.

"What are you doing here dressed like that at this time of night?" She huffed and pulled her cardigan closed as she leaned forward to glance through her gate, which she had yet to unlock. "You look like a Peridale lass."

"I got on the wrong bus," Julia explained, which wasn't technically a lie. "End of the line."

The woman rolled her eyes and tutted. That was all she needed to produce a key to unlock the gate. She swung it open and motioned for Julia to hurry inside.

"Busses weren't like that in my day," she said with a shake of her mousy, frizzy curls. "They'd take you right to your door if you really needed it, but now they'd drop you off in the middle of nowhere and charge you an arm and a leg for it."

"£4.90."

"*Gordon Bennett*!" she cried as she locked the gate and door behind them. "Thank heavens I'm a pensioner with a free bus pass! I'm Addie. I know you told me your name, but the old memory isn't what it used to be."

"Julia," she repeated. "Julia South-Brown."

"Then take a seat, Julia, and make yourself comfortable." Addie steered Julia into a floral armchair by an electric fire. "I'll make you a nice pot of tea with lots of sugar. You're probably in shock."

Julia settled into the warmth of Addie's flat, and, for a moment, she almost forgot why she was there. The walls were pale pink, the carpet was dark pink, and the sofa and armchair were patterned with shades of pink flowers. Porcelain ornaments and framed photographs balanced on a narrow fireplace above the electric fire. It was as snug and homey as a flat in Fern Moore could get.

"J-Julia?" a male voice broke the silence. "What are you doing here?"

Julia allowed herself to breathe a sigh of relief when Oliver shuffled out of one of the bedrooms in pyjamas and a long dressing gown. She said a silent thank you to Johnny for not leading her astray.

"Ah, Oliver!" Addie shuffled out of the kitchen with a tray containing a large teapot with two china cups and half a Battenberg cake. "This is Julia. She's in a spot of trouble. Fern Moore thugs."

"Are you all right?" Oliver asked, his voice filled with genuine concern.

Julia's naked left hand rested on her chest where the locket usually sat. "I'll be fine. It's good to see you again, Oliver."

"Oh, you know each other?" Addie asked as she placed the tray on the low coffee table. "It's a small world, isn't it?"

Julia decided against repeating that she had mentioned she had knocked on the door looking for someone. Addie's kindness was too great to have Julia insult her declining memory.

Oliver perched on the sofa opposite to Julia in the armchair. He looked uneasy but no more anxious than he'd looked at the bake-off.

"Let me grab another cup," Addie said. "Help

yourselves to the cake."

Oliver and Julia eyed up the cake before their eyes met. Julia offered a smile, but Oliver's eyes darted away to the television, which was silently playing *Emmerdale* with the subtitles on.

"Johnny told me I could find you here," Julia said. "I wasn't planning on turning up like this, but—well, I didn't have much choice. How are you holding up? I've been worried about you."

"You have?"

"Of course," Julia assured him. "What happened on Sunday was a lot for anyone to deal with."

"Life's not fair." Oliver shrugged. "I learned that young."

Addie hurried back in and added another cup and saucer to the tray. She filled the cups, leaving room for milk. Without asking Julia if she wanted sugar, she added three generous scoops.

"Now, I won't have you not having a slice of cake," Addie said as she cut a thick piece. "It's only shop-bought, but who's judging?"

Julia and Oliver's eyes met, and for whatever reason, they both started laughing at the same moment.

"What's so funny?" Addie asked, joining in the

laughter as she handed Julia the cake.

"Julia was the other judge at the bake-off," Oliver said.

"And that's funny?"

"You said no one would be judging your cake, but Julia was there to judge cakes." Oliver waved his hand. "She runs a café. It doesn't matter."

"*Oh*!" Addie snatched the plate from Julia. "In that case, I won't have you eating this muck! Let me see what else I have. I think I have some of my Christmas cake left over from December."

"You really don't have—"

"I'll have none of that!" Addie put Julia's plate back on the tray, took off the teapot and the teacups, and picked it up. "Only the best for a judge. I won't embarrass myself with a Battenberg from the corner shop!"

Leaving them alone again, Addie whizzed off to the kitchen.

"So, this is what other people's grandmothers are like?" Julia asked. "Mine is somewhat of a special case."

"Addie isn't my grandmother," Oliver corrected her. "I just rent her spare bedroom. She put an advert for a lodger in the post office window in Riverswick. I saw it when I was buying Mr

Bridges' lunch. I couldn't have ended up with a nicer landlady. She's as close to family as I have right now."

"What about Johnny?"

"What about him?"

"He's your cousin."

"My mum is his mum's half-sister," Oliver said, as though they weren't the same thing. "That's as far as the family connection stretches. Johnny's mum hates my mum and vice versa. I've barely had more than a couple of conversations with Johnny or his sister in my whole life."

"Where's your mother now?"

Oliver shrugged. "Travelling, I think. Haven't heard from her in a couple of years. She never stays in one place for too long."

"Are you talking about that mother of yours?" Addie called as she brought in three thick slices of Christmas cake. "Waste of space! Women like her don't deserve the miracle of children. Can you imagine having a child and then palming him off on strangers so you can gallop around the place doing heaven knows what?"

"What about your dad?" Julia asked.

Oliver shrugged, and this time didn't follow it up with a comment. She wondered if that shrug meant he didn't know where he was either, or if he didn't know who he was at all. The sadness in Oliver's eyes made a lot more sense to Julia. Tony might have been treating him like rubbish, but that wasn't where his pain started and ended.

"Now, you have to tell me what you think." Addie perched on the chair's arm and stared at the cake in Julia's lap. "I fed it brandy for a whole year!"

Julia forked off a chunk of the heavy Christmas cake. It was moist with an even distribution of fruit, and appeared to be perfect, even if the brandy scent was more pungent than Julia would have expected. She placed it in her mouth and had to use all her strength not to cough when the alcohol hit the back of her throat.

"It's got a kick!" Julia mumbled as she chewed. "You can really taste the brandy."

"Oh, I'm so glad you like it." Addie finally sat down on the sofa next to Oliver. "It's an old family recipe passed down from my great-grandparents, although I suppose it will die with me as I have no one to pass it to." Addie stared at the television for a moment before snapping her fingers and scurrying off once again.

"You get used to it," Oliver said with a sweet smile. "She's all over the place, but her heart is in everything she does. Believe it or not, this is Addie on a good day. It's going to be hard to leave."

"Where are you going?"

"I don't know." Oliver huffed and collapsed fully into the floral sofa. "I have enough money to cover next month's rent, but if I don't have another job by then, I'm back to sofa surfing. I know Addie would let me stay here for nothing if I was desperate, but I wouldn't do that to her. She's on a pension, and she doesn't need me hiking up her bills."

"I'm sure you'll find something."

"Without a reference?" Oliver took a big bite of the strong cake. "Unless I can contact Mr Bridges via a Ouija board, my time with him is as good as useless. I only got that job down to luck."

Addie hurried back in brandishing a yellowed piece of paper with faded pencil markings.

"My old family recipe for the Christmas cake," she announced as she wrapped Julia's hand around the sheet. "I want you to have it."

"Me?"

"There's no better custodian than a baking judge!" Addie said with a satisfied nod as she sat down again. "Just make sure to follow the steps exactly and promise you'll make it every year."

"I don't think I can—"

"I just wrote down a copy, dear." Addie waved her hand before scooping up the remote control and clicking through the channels. "Now, hush up. *Eastenders* is on."

Oliver gave Julia a smile to let her know this was the usual evening routine. They sat in complete silence while the East London soap played silently on the small television, with only the subtitles to help them follow the story. Julia sipped her sweet tea, and as the sugar washed over her, she struggled to remember any life outside Addie's pink flat.

"What's that racket outside?" Addie sighed, rolling her eyes at the window. "There's always someone screaming and shouting around here!"

Julia continued reading the subtitles until she thought she heard her name. She strained her ears, and again, she heard her name on the wind. She practically tossed the cup onto the side table when she recognised Barker's voice. She darted around the sofa and rattled the chain off before yanking the door open.

"You'll need the key," Addie said as she slowly wandered over, her eyes still on the television while she reached into her nightie's pocket to produce a large key. "I never leave the thing unlocked. They'd have my carpets up if they could! Take anything that's not nailed down."

Addie unlocked the gate and swung it open for Julia. She ran out and almost threw herself over the edge of the balcony. She had never been more relieved to see Jessie's yellow car.

"*Julia!*" Jessie yelled, hands cupping her mouth as she circled the now empty park. "*Julia!*"

"*I'm up here!*" she cried, waving her arms.

Barker and Jessie looked up, and even though they were three floors down, she was sure she heard them let out a collective breath.

"*Stay there!*" Barker called, pointing at her. "I'm coming up."

Julia backed away from the balcony, and for the first time since arriving in Fern Moore, she felt truly safe. While she waited for Barker to run up the stairwell, Julia walked back into Addie's flat. The little old lady was already back on the sofa, her eyes glued to the silent soap.

"Thank you for looking after me," Julia called over the back of the sofa. "My husband is here, so I'll get out of your hair. Thanks for the tea and cake. I really appreciate your help, Addie."

"No problem, dear." Addie waved over her

shoulder without looking away from the screen. "Drop by again."

Julia wondered if Addie even remembered who she was or why she was there, but she was grateful all the same. She turned to leave the flat once and for all, but a hand closed around her arm.

"I need to tell you something," Oliver whispered, clutching something plastic and yellow in his hand. "I found this."

"Tony's EpiPen!"

"I didn't kill him," Oliver said quickly, "if that's what you're thinking. I didn't."

"Why do you have it?"

"I told you, I found it." Oliver glanced at Addie and pulled Julia towards the door and out of earshot. "When Tony died, I freaked out. I was pacing the tent, and I saw this poking out from under Tony's coat on the floor. I panicked, and I picked it up. I don't know why, and I don't know why I didn't say something then, but the longer I held onto it in my pocket, the worse I knew it would look."

"I'm not going to lie to you, Oliver. This doesn't look good."

"I know." He chewed into his lip as he held out the EpiPen. "I know how this looks, but I didn't take it; I found it when it was too late for it to make a difference. Are you going to tell the police?"

Julia considered if she would, but she wasn't sure what difference it would make. If Oliver was telling the truth about finding it after Tony had been pronounced dead, he was right about the EpiPen not making a difference.

"I won't tell them," Julia started, resting her hand on his shoulder, "but I want you to do something for me in return."

"What?"

"Meet me at my café tomorrow night," she said. "Around six. It'll be closed, but I'll be there."

"W-what are we going to do?" Oliver gulped. "I'm not sure—"

"By the sounds of it, Tony didn't have many people he was close to," Julia said, cutting him off before his imagination ran away with him. "You followed Tony around, bending to his every whim. I'm going to bet you heard and saw things you shouldn't have. I need your help to try to build a clearer picture of the man so I can figure out who would want to kill him, and, more importantly, why."

"You sound like police. I thought you ran a café?" Oliver asked, his expression confused.

"I do. I'll see you tomorrow night at six."

Leaving Oliver with the EpiPen, Julia exited the flat and pushed the gate back into place. Barker and Jessie emerged at the end of the walkway, practically fighting past each other to get to her. Jessie reached her first and wrapped her arms tightly around Julia's neck.

"You're okay," Jessie whispered into Julia's chest. "You're okay."

"How did you know I was here?"

"Dot's message," Barker said as he wrapped his arms around the two of them.

"She figured out how to use her machine?"

"No, but Percy did." Barker kissed Julia on the top of the head. "I think it's time we took you home and had a chat, don't you?"

Agatha Frost

9

After a hot shower and a much-needed cup of peppermint and liquorice tea, Julia collapsed into her armchair next to the roaring fire. They had collected Vinnie from Dot and Percy, and he now slept soundly in his cot in the bedroom.

Mowgli jumped up onto Julia's lap and kneaded her pink dressing gown before curling up. On the surface, it could have been an ordinary Thursday night at home, but the atmosphere was far from ordinary.

"Christie is on his way." Barker emerged from the bedroom holding his phone. "He's going to take your statement and get started on catching those thugs."

"I said I'd do it in the morning." Julia rested her head on the back of the chair and closed her eyes as the fire warmed her feet. "I'm so tired. I just want to relax."

"Relax?" Barker cried. "*Relax*?"

"Keep your voice down! You're going to wake Vinnie."

"A crying baby is the least of your worries right now, Julia!" Barker paced behind the sofa, his hands in his hair. "You were *mugged*! Do you have any idea what it felt like to get that call from Dot?"

"Barker, I—"

"I assumed the *worst*!" His voice grew louder. "When we arrived, and you weren't near the phone box, my mind went to a horrid place. Do you know how many murders start with a mugging? *Do you*, Julia? Because I do. I lived that life for too many years when I worked in the city."

"And Peridale isn't the city."

"And Fern Moore *isn't* Peridale." He stopped pacing and tossed his arms out, his eyes pinning

Julia into the chair. "I don't care about official borders and postcodes. That place isn't like this village, not even on Peridale's worst day. The people who live there are not like *us*."

"They're not all like that, Barker." Julia pursed her lips. "Addie, for one. And what about Billy? He came from there too."

"And what about the rest? What about the ones who mugged you? Nice people don't snatch the rings off your hand!" Barker deflated and leaned against the back of the sofa. "I'm sorry. I think I'm in shock."

"I was the one who had to live through it," Julia reminded him.

"Which is why I don't understand how you're so calm." Barker walked around the sofa and sat down. Mowgli sprang off Julia's lap and ran into the bedroom, allowing Barker to grab Julia's hands in his. "What were you doing in Fern Moore? I left you miles away at a children's soft play area to talk to Bev."

"And that's what I did. I spoke to her, and I ended up on a bus."

"What were you doing on a bus?"

"I wanted to talk to Bev without her thinking I was prying answers from her," Julia explained before yawning. "It worked. She opened up, and I got a lot of useful information from her."

"Useful information?" Barker let go of Julia's hands and collapsed into the sofa. He covered his face as he breathed heavily. "Maybe you're also in shock and not processing what happened. This isn't a game, Julia. You're not playing Cluedo and trying to pin it on Professor Plum in the library with the candlestick. This is *real* life! You have too many people who care about you to be throwing yourself into dangerous situations like this."

Julia's first instinct was to jump to her own defence. In the two years they'd known each other, Barker had never spoken to Julia like this before, and as she stared into his eyes and saw his fear, she understood why.

"Barker, I don't know what to say—"

"Promise me you won't throw yourself into a situation like that again." Barker sounded more exhausted than Julia felt. "Do you remember what I told you about Vanessa?"

Julia was taken aback to hear that name leave Barker's lips. In their first few months of dating, Barker had told her about being briefly engaged to a woman called Vanessa, an officer shot to death by a lunatic who wanted to exact revenge on the police after being arrested for driving while drunk. Barker hadn't mentioned her since that night, and Julia hadn't known how to ask about it, so she hadn't.

"I remember," she said softly.

"It's been almost ten years." Barker let his hands run down his face. "I don't mean to bring her up. You're my wife, and I love you more than anyone I've ever known, but—"

"You can talk about anything with me, Barker." Julia got out of the chair and sat next to him. She clutched his hands in hers. "Anything."

"Vanessa was a police officer murdered at random by someone angry about losing their license." Barker paused and turned to look at Julia with a firm gaze. "Do you know what that means? If someone is willing to murder a police officer for something as trivial as that, what do you think a maniac is going to do to an ordinary person for their phone and jewellery?"

"They were kids."

"Did they have a weapon?"

"Barker, I—"

"Did they have a *weapon*?" Barker repeated. "Because I know you, Julia, and I know you wouldn't have handed over your mother's ring unless you really had to."

Julia nodded, which caused Barker to cover his face again. He didn't ask what the weapon was, and there was a knock at the door before he had a chance to.

"That will be Christie," Barker said, dragging himself off the couch. "I'll let him in."

Julia resumed her place in her armchair and took a gulp of her tea for courage. Jessie emerged from her bedroom and took the wonky armchair next to the window. Julia tried to catch her eye, but she seemed to be having as hard a time as Barker. Julia had been through a whole range of emotions since the mugging, but she hadn't expected guilt to be one of them, and yet it consumed her more than any other.

"Julia." DI Christie nodded to her as he sat on the sofa. "I'm sorry to hear about what happened. There are some real low lives out there. Barker told me most of the story over the phone, but I want to hear it from you first-hand. Start at the beginning."

Christie pulled out a notepad, and for the first time since Julia had met him, he seemed genuinely concerned for her welfare. The mocking glare was gone from his eyes, and his usual smirk was downturned at the corners.

Julia started with the visit to the soft play area, and then the chance meeting with Bev. She was honest about why she wanted to talk to her. She recounted the bus journey to Fern Moore, where she had planned to get a taxi. She explained that Johnny had sent her a text, and before she could call anyone, the gang appeared. When she mentioned the knife, Barker let out a pained sigh and continued pacing in the hallway. Jessie's fists clenched against the armchair, her top lip curled in a snarl as she stared into the fireplace.

"You did the right thing not putting up a fight." Christie slapped the pad shut when she finished the story. "Too many innocent people have died trying to protect their possessions. We can't take them with us to the other side, right?" He stood and tucked the pad into his jacket pocket. "Look, Julia, I'm going to be honest with you. It's very unlikely that we're going to find your items. I'll put an alert out to all the pawn shops in the area. If those thugs are stupid enough, they'll try to trade them in, but those types are usually savvier than that. They know how to get rid of things without anyone ever finding out."

"Don't forget the bus," Barker injected. "It

might have had cameras."

"Good point." Christie made a note of it. "I'll call the company first thing. You've given us some good stuff to work with. I know a couple of guys by the name of Mark who hang around the estate, so I'll do my best."

"Thank you, Detective," Julia said after stifling another yawn. "I'm sorry to make you come out so late. I appreciate it."

"No problem." Christie walked into the hallway and patted Barker on the back before looking back into the sitting room. "Julia?"

"Yes?"

"I'm going to say this for your own good and not to score points." Christie's eyes darted down to the floor as he seemed to be arranging his words. "Please, for your sake, you need to stop investigating. You're a clever woman, but I'd hate for you to die trying to outdo me." He paused. "You run rings around Barker and me when it comes to this. Maybe you're in the wrong profession, and you'd be better suited at the station, but please, stick to the baking. I couldn't live with myself if something happened to you."

Christie patted Barker on the shoulder again and left the cottage, leaving a cloud of stuffy silence in his wake. Julia had solved countless mysteries over the past couple of years, but for the first time, she asked herself if it was worth what she stood to lose.

"I think I need to go to bed," Julia said, unable to look at either of them as she stood. "I really am sorry."

Barker kissed her on the cheek as she passed, but he didn't follow her. Julia climbed under the covers and stared through the open curtains at the sharp crescent moon in the pitch-black sky. Despite her exhaustion, she was still awake when Barker climbed into bed during the early hours of the morning. He wrapped himself around her and clung like he had never clung before.

10

Julia slept in until three in the afternoon the next day. When she first opened her eyes, she thought she'd only slept for a couple of hours, which made looking at the clock and seeing that she'd almost slept for a solid twelve all the more shocking. She let out a yawn, feeling like she could fall back asleep if she stayed in bed any longer.

She tossed back the covers, noticing how light her hand felt without the rings she'd grown so used to. She touched her neck; another bare space where something precious had once sat.

"They're things," Julia muttered as she stuffed her feet into her sheepskin slippers. "You're not a materialistic woman."

With heavy steps and a sleepy mind, Julia plodded to her bedroom door in the late afternoon gloom, feeling like Jessie looked most mornings. She scratched her head and fought back a series of all-consuming yawns.

"You're awake," Barker called cheerfully from the kitchen. "I was just making you some breakfast."

"It's three in the afternoon," Julia said, checking the cat clock above the fridge to make sure her alarm clock hadn't lied to her. "Why did you let me sleep that long?"

"Because you needed it." Barker scooped bacon onto a plate, which contained a full English breakfast fit for a queen. "Jessie insisted she run the café on her own today, so I turned off your alarm when you didn't wake up with me this morning."

"Where's Vinnie?"

"With Dot and Percy," Barker said as he ushered Julia onto a stool at the counter. "Everything is taken care of. You don't have to worry. Do you want your tea?"

"Coffee," Julia found herself saying. "I need it."

Barker put the plate in front of Julia along with a knife and fork, a napkin, and a bottle of ketchup. He quickly made a cup of coffee and placed it next to her as she started working on her two fried eggs. Barker wasn't an unromantic man, but he'd never gone to such lengths before.

"Is it good?"

"It's really nice," Julia mumbled through a mouthful of sausage. "I'm very grateful for this, and, not to sound rude, but what's the occasion?"

"Can't I make my wife a full English now and then?" Barker's fake plastered smile melted away after a couple of seconds. "Okay, it's an apology. The way I acted yesterday was out of line."

"Oh, Barker—"

"No, Julia." Barker held his hand up. "You were right. You had to live through it. I didn't. I was upset and scared, and I took it out on you, the last person who should have had to deal with it after going through something like that."

"I'm honestly fine," Julia said, and she meant it. "It's already yesterday's news. I can't do anything to change what happened. I got myself into that situation, and I lived to talk about it. The chances of it happening again are probably statistically low right now, right?"

"Technically, yes." Barker grabbed a plastic bag from next to the sink and reached inside. "But it doesn't mean you don't have to be prepared. It's better to be safe than sorry, yes?"

"I suppose." Julia squinted at the bag as she took a bite out of her buttery toast. "What's in the bag?"

"I went to the shopping centre and picked up a few things." Barker reached into the bag and pulled out a small white box. "A state-of-the-art mobile phone to replace the stolen one. It was a little pricey, but the man in the shop said I could link it up with mine and we can track each other at all times."

Julia took a silent bite out of her toast as she watched Barker retrieve the next item.

"A panic alarm." He placed another box on the counter. "And a whistle. I've always said every woman should carry these around, but few actually do."

"What next?" Julia mumbled through bacon. "Pepper spray?"

"Well, yes." Barker pulled out a black canister. "Christie did me a favour and took one from the station's inventory. He signed it out so no one will miss it."

Julia choked on her bacon as she stared at the police-grade weapon.

"Barker, I'm sure it's illegal to carry that!"

"It is." Barker winked. "But who's going to know?"

"And what if I use it?" Julia wiped her mouth with a napkin. "I'll be arrested for using a dangerous weapon. You of all people should know that. It's illegal for you to be holding that right now. You're a civilian like the rest of us."

Barker tapped the spray against his chin. "I never looked at it like that. Okay, we'll keep the spray in the house for emergencies."

As she watched Barker dig around in the bag for his next item, Julia suddenly had no appetite. She pushed the plate away and gulped down more coffee to wake her mind fully.

"A flashlight," Barker said, holding out a small torch for Julia. "An essential."

"Don't tell me, does it turn into a bomb if I twist it a certain way?"

"No, it's just very bright." Barker shone the torch in Julia's eyes, and she almost fell backwards off her stool. "Good for dazzling people."

Julia regained her balance as she blinked away stars; if she hadn't been awake before, she was now.

"Last but not least." Barker pulled out the final item. "A Swiss army knife. Before you ask, it's legal to carry this around as long as you keep the blade retracted." He flipped the blade out to show Julia how it worked before slotting it back. "Of course, if you use it, that's another story, but hopefully it doesn't get to that. If you haven't scared them off with all this other stuff, a flash of this thing should do it."

Julia was somewhere between touched and dumbfounded as she stared at the counter full of self-defence items. "Barker, I'm touched, but don't you think this is a little extreme?"

"It's better to be—"

"Safe than sorry," Julia jumped in. "I know, and in theory, that's a lovely idea, but do you really expect me to carry all this around with me every time I leave the house? My bag is small!"

"Well, you just need a bigger bag."

"I'd need an overnight bag for all this." Julia reached across the counter and rested her hand on Barker's. "Thank you, but you need to trust that I'll be okay. The world is a scary place, but I refuse to live in fear of it, and neither should you."

"I only want you to be safe."

"But where does that end?" Julia chuckled. "I start wearing stab vests and riot gear to pop down to the shop when we're out of milk?"

"Now that's an idea." Barker assessed his haul. "Perhaps I went a little overboard."

"Perhaps a little." Julia cast her eyes over the items before plucking out the torch, whistle, and alarm. "I'll take these, okay? The rest can stay in the house. And please, give Christie that pepper spray back. It's not worth breaking the law for."

"And what if we're burgled in the middle of the night?"

"There's a pepper grinder in the cupboard." Julia stuffed the items into her handbag. "Improvise."

Leaving Barker to clean up the mess he'd made in the kitchen, Julia carried her new phone through to the sitting room. It took a full hour to set it up. When she had everyone's phone numbers transferred from Barker's phone, she sent all her contacts a message to let them know she had a new number. Johnny, Roxy, and Leah texted back immediately with similar messages along the lines of 'is it true you were mugged last night?'

"How do you text three people the same message?" Julia asked Barker. "I don't know how many ways I can explain this without sounding repetitive."

"Jessie showed me how to do group messages." Barker pressed a couple of things on Julia's screen, merging the messages with Roxy, Johnny, and Leah into one. "There. Now you can all talk together."

Julia didn't know how, but her friends seemed to know they were now all in one chat together. They bombarded her with messages, one after the other.

"Barker, I want my old phone back." Julia held the device out as it beeped with each new message. "This is too complicated."

"You'll get the hang of it. If you ever feel like you've had enough of the messages, just click that button on the side. It will put it all on silent."

Julia clicked the button, and the beeping stopped, but the messages kept coming through. She quickly typed a response:

Yes, it's true, but don't worry, I'm fine. It will take more than a bunch of kids to stop me. Will explain later when I see you all! Please don't worry about me (and stop with all the messages. Still getting used to the new phone haha) x

Julia pressed something on the keyboard, and the letters turned into tiny pictures. She sent a laughing crying face, a ghost with its tongue out, and a thumbs up. Leah and Roxy both sent back the same confused face, but Johnny sent a yellow grinning face donning a cowboy hat.

After calling the bank to cancel her cards, which thankfully hadn't been used after all, Julia showered and dressed. By the time she put her shoes on, it was already past five, and the sun had started to set. It felt strange to start her day so late, but she had promised to meet Oliver, and she wasn't going to stand him up.

"I'm going to help Jessie clean up the café," Julia called into the dining room while Barker caught up on the work he'd missed while shopping for weapons. "She's been doing too much on her own."

"Be safe."

"I will." Julia waved her new phone in the air. "I'm taking my car, anyway. No getting stranded this time. I shouldn't be too long. After we've finished with the café, I'll collect Vinnie and come back. Figure out what we're having for dinner if you get a minute. I haven't had time to go shopping, but the freezer is full."

"Yep," Barker said, barely looking up from his typewriter. "Will do."

Leaving him to his work, Julia drove into the village and parked behind Jessie's car next to her café. She was glad most of the customers had already left because she wasn't sure how far word of her mugging had spread, but when Evelyn's eyes landed on her, she knew most people in the village likely already knew.

"*Julia!*" Evelyn cried. "Oh, poor Julia! I've been trying to call you!"

"I have a new phone number." Julia patted her bag. "Is everything okay?"

"Oh, not over the phone! I was trying to call you *psychically*, and it seems to have worked because *here* you are!"

"I suppose it did." Julia chuckled as Jessie circled her finger around her head behind Evelyn's back. "I'm going to assume you've heard."

"*Heard?*" Evelyn exclaimed, fanning herself dramatically. "I *foresaw* it! Moments before it happened, I saw something sinister in the tea leaves. I didn't know who the warning pertained to, but I knew it was someone I cared deeply about.

Unfortunately, it was *you*, Julia! I do *wish* I could have forewarned you in some way."

"I wish I could have forewarned myself." Julia unbuttoned her coat and rolled the sleeves of her jumper up. "If you don't mind, Evelyn, I'm going to help Jessie close up now. Make sure to tell people you saw me, and I was completely fine."

"I will radiate that message around the village," Evelyn said as she floated to the door. "Take care of yourself, Julia. We're ten days away from a full moon. I predict stranger things will happen in this village before then. Goodbye!"

Evelyn hurried out of the café, leaving Julia to lock the door behind her.

"I wish she'd predict something *before* bad things happened for once," Jessie muttered as she began clearing the day's unsold cakes out of the display case. "She's always the first to swoop in and say she foresaw it, but she never knocks on your door to deliver the bad news, just to say, 'I told you so!'"

"She's harmless."

"She's *batty*!"

"I believe that she believes, and that's enough for me." Julia rested her hand on Jessie's shoulder. "Is there anything you want to talk about?"

"No. Why would there be?"

"I don't know," Julia lied, her mind casting back to what Dot and Percy claimed to have seen on Mulberry Lane. "Anything at all. I'm always here to listen if you need to talk."

The silence that followed dragged out until Julia realised Jessie wasn't going to respond. They cleaned the café in silence, each doing a deeper clean than they usually would on a Friday night. When the café was gleaming in every corner, Julia had ten minutes to spare before Oliver's arrival— not that she was sure he'd turn up at all.

"You can go home," Julia said. "I'll finish up here."

"But we're finished." Jessie frowned. "And you've boxed my car in."

"Then I'll move it."

"You never want to stay behind and clean on your own." Jessie stepped to the side to stop Julia grabbing her car keys from her bag. "You're still sleuthing, aren't you?"

"No," Julia said quickly. "Maybe. I don't know. I'm meeting a kid called Oliver. He's in a pretty bad place. He was Tony Bridges' assistant, and I want to see if he knows anything that could help flesh out why someone would want to kill Tony. That's all. He's not dangerous. He's about your age."

"Those thugs last night were about my age," Jessie replied flatly. "If you're meeting this guy, I'm staying behind."

"Okay."

"*Okay*?"

"If that's what you want to do, then okay." Julia wrapped her arm around Jessie's shoulders. "Just remember that I'm here for you, just like you're always here for me."

Julia held her breath and waited for Jessie to reveal what was going on with her, but no revelations came.

"Don't make it weird, cake lady." Jessie shrugged off Julia's arm and started making herself a coffee. "I'm staying to make sure he's not a psycho killer."

***

When Oliver turned up at the café at 6pm on the dot, Julia knew she'd had no reason to doubt him. He'd been honest about finding the EpiPen, and now he was here to help her.

"Do you want anything to eat or drink?" Julia asked from behind the counter as Oliver hovered in the middle of the café clutching a laptop bag. "I can make almost any drink you can imagine, and there's a fridge full of cakes in the kitchen."

"No, thank you."

"You can say yes." Julia tried her best to look as disarming as she could. "I'm not going to bite, Oliver."

"I might," Jessie added as she pulled out a chair for Oliver to sit in.

"She won't," Julia said when she saw the fear in Oliver's eyes. "She's joking."

"I'm not."

"She is."

Jessie leaned into Oliver's ear and whispered, "*I'm not.*"

Julia shook her head at Jessie and gave her a look that she hoped read 'leave the kid alone!', to which Jessie rolled her eyes before sitting at the table next to Oliver. Despite his protests, Julia made him a cinnamon latte and plated up a chocolate-topped cream choux bun.

After making her own cup of tea, Julia sat across the table from Oliver and watched as he tucked into the choux bun. Her baking often acted as the perfect icebreaker. Regardless of how Jessie was glaring at him, he appeared to relax.

"Are you ready to talk about Tony?" Julia prompted after sipping her tea. "Take your time and tell me anything you can about him, whether you think it's useful or not."

"I could spend hours *telling* you what an awful man Mr Bridges was, but you already know that." Oliver reached into his bag and pulled out a beat-up old laptop covered in stickers. "Or, I could *show* you what I found last night. When you said you wanted to talk to me about Mr Bridges, I didn't know what I could tell you that you hadn't already witnessed. The Mr Bridges I experienced was the Mr Bridges you—"

"Are you going to call him *Mr* Bridges the *whole* time?" Jessie jumped in. "Because if so, that's going to get really annoying. The man is dead. He can't fire you. Call him Tony."

"Fine." Oliver shot Jessie a cold look. "Tony was the man he came across as. I worked for him for a whole year, and I never saw another side to him. I went to bed dreading waking up because I knew I'd have to spend another day walking on eggshells."

"If it was that bad, why didn't you just quit?" Jessie asked with a roll of her eyes.

"Because I didn't have a choice," Oliver fired

back, growing in confidence with every word. "I didn't grow up with a family who had a business. I didn't grow up—"

"Neither did I," Jessie cut him off. "I was orphaned before I could walk or talk. I didn't have anything handed to me. I was homeless when Julia first met me, so don't give me that nonsense. You always have a choice. You chose to stay working for him. And even if it was only for the money that's still a choice."

"Okay, so it was a *choice*." Oliver exhaled as he typed on the laptop. "The point is, Tony was awful around the clock, and I was usually with him around the clock. I had to go everywhere with him every day, and I usually ended up sitting in the corner for hours on end until he needed me."

"Is this going somewhere?" Jessie asked before yawning. "My bed is calling."

"*Jessie*!" Julia snapped. "You don't have to stay."

"I'm not yet convinced he's not going to kill you," Jessie said after another yawn. "Continue, kid, just get to the point."

"Fine." Oliver typed something else before spinning his laptop around. "The point is, two months ago, Tony's laptop broke, and he insisted on using mine. He only gave it me back last week. I had to save for months to buy that thing. He could have bought a new one, but that's how little he cared about me. I told him how important that laptop was to me, but he ignored me. He only gave it me back because I told Camila and she bought him a new one."

"The *point*?" Jessie pushed again.

"The point is, he left his emails logged in, and I don't even think he realised it." Oliver pushed the laptop to Julia. "I didn't realise it until last night. When you mentioned you wanted information on Tony, I searched my laptop to see if he'd left any trace of his activities. He'd saved his email password to my laptop on the first login, and let's just say the man had no idea how to clear a search history."

"Have you gone through them?" Julia asked as she scrolled through the endless emails.

"I haven't slept." Oliver offered a sheepish smile. "The ones with the stars next to them are the ones I thought were important. I always knew Tony had a screw or two loose, but I never realised how paranoid he was."

"Paranoid how?" Jessie asked, her interest captured.

"Well, for a start, he sent twenty-three emails

to the Cotswold Baking Society confirming his peanut allergy." Oliver leaned over the screen and pointed to some as Julia scrolled. "Look at the subjects. 'URGENT!', 'IMPORTANT!', 'PLEASE RESPOND!' I read them all, and they were all just him confirming and reconfirming that they knew about his allergy. They replied the same things over and over, but he never seemed satisfied. And it doesn't end there. He thought he was being followed."

"By whom?" Julia asked.

"Everyone." Oliver pulled the laptop from Julia and opened a folder of images. "I downloaded all these from the emails. There are over three hundred images that he took of people he thought were following him. Only two people pop up in more than one image; the rest are random people in the lines at coffee shops and people behind him in the supermarket."

"Who were the people following him?" Julia asked as she squinted at the thumbnails.

"Well, I think you already know one of them." Oliver double clicked on an image, and it popped up to fill the screen. "Bev, his ex-wife. There were dozens of pictures of her outside their house, but they were all dated within a twelve-month period, and the last one was over a year ago. The other person was more recent." Oliver clicked on another picture. "This guy actually seems to have been following Tony, unless it's a coincidence that he popped up in all these pictures in the last six months. The most recent one was taken the day before the bake-off." Oliver clicked on another picture to show the same man standing in a public bathroom. "It looks like Tony was hiding in the stall."

"Who is he?" Jessie asked.

"I don't know," Oliver admitted. "I saw him a couple of times, but I thought Tony was just making it up. He liked to pretend he was more famous than he was and having people obsessed enough to follow him gave him an ego boost."

"Who was he sending these emails to?" Julia asked.

"That's the weird part," Oliver said. "Until last year, he was sending them to his lawyer, but I found an email from the lawyer telling him they were no longer working with him because Tony hadn't paid his bills for months. Since then, he emailed himself with the same subject in them all."

Oliver clicked back onto the emails and then typed one word in the search bar. *PROOF*. Eighty-nine emails popped up, all with image attachments. Julia opened a couple, and the same guy popped up in almost all of them.

"A stalker, maybe?" Jessie suggested. "Or a crazy fan?"

"Either way, I almost feel bad that I never believed he was really being followed, but this proves it." Oliver leaned back in his chair. "Maybe if I'd listened—"

"He would still have been an unbearable idiot," Jessie jumped in. "Don't feel too bad."

Oliver smiled at Jessie, and she smiled back. Oliver reminded Julia of Jessie when they'd first met; full of fear and confused by the world around him.

"This is all really good stuff," Julia said, patting the laptop. "I'm not sure what it means, but something was going on. Is there anything else in here?"

"Aside from him emailing the radio station once a month to ask for a pay rise, nothing out of the ordinary." Oliver pulled the laptop back towards him.

"I know it's a long shot, but can you forward me all of his emails and the images?" Julia asked, her fingers drumming on the table as she mulled over the information. "If it's not too much trouble?"

"It's already compressed into a folder and attached to an email," Oliver replied. "I just need your email address."

After Julia handed over her address, and Jessie promised to help her figure out how to 'un-compress' the file on the other end, Oliver finished his coffee and packed up his laptop. When Julia glanced at the clock, she was surprised to see that they had been talking for an hour.

"I should go." Oliver slung his bag over his shoulder. "I don't like to leave Addie on her own at this time of night. She starts to get a little odd when the sun goes down. Caught her trying to put her slippers in the toaster last week. Do you know if the bus to Fern Moore goes through here?"

"No busses." Jessie walked over to the counter and grabbed her keys. "I'll give you a lift."

"You don't—"

"It's no trouble." Jessie pushed Oliver towards the door. "I've decided you're probably not a psycho killer."

"Only probably?"

"There's still time."

"Take care of yourself, Oliver," Julia called after

him. "You know where I am if you need me."

"Thank you." Oliver paused while Jessie held the door open for him. "There's one more thing, actually. I didn't understand it at the time, and I still don't, but I overheard Mr—I mean, I overheard *Tony* on the phone four days ago. He said something about a horse and being sued. It doesn't make much sense, but it stuck in my mind, so I thought I'd mention it."

"No, it makes perfect sense," Julia said, almost to herself. "Take care."

After gathering up her things, Julia pulled out her new phone and opened the search engine. She typed 'Horses Peridale' into the search bar, and clicked on the first result that came up, a riding school called Peridale Riding Centre. Julia didn't have to go any further than the 'OUR TEAM' page to see the face she wanted. The horse-scented coffee-slinger from the morning of the bake-off now had a name and a title: 'Florence Henshaw - Owner.'

11

Julia planned to visit the riding school with Vinnie on Saturday, but heavy rain thwarted her. Instead, Barker looked after Vinnie at the cottage while Julia worked with Jessie at the café all day. Thanks to Dot's big mouth and the gossip channels, every customer knew about Julia's mugging, although most of what they had heard had been highly exaggerated along the way. Julia couldn't believe what she was saying when she had to assure Father David that the attacker hadn't been carrying a machete, and she was even more in disbelief when she had to tell Shilpa she hadn't hospitalised three of them with her bare hands.

Late on Saturday night, Dot called Julia in a panic, insisting that they meet for lunch on Sunday afternoon. She assured her it was an emergency, but since she wouldn't impart the information over the phone, Julia concluded that it couldn't have been that important.

"Can I pick the venue?" Julia had asked.

"Yes, dear," Dot had replied. "Just make sure to invite your sister, too. It's important!"

When they pulled into Little Tots Treasures' car park on Sunday afternoon, Dot looked less than impressed.

"A children's play area?" Dot cried as they pulled into one of the free spaces at the back of the car park. "Have you lost your marbles, Julia? I said *lunch*, not *torture*!"

"It's not so bad. They serve coffee."

"So does prison! Doesn't mean I want to go there either."

Despite Dot's upset, Vinnie seemed to remember where he was, and he bounced and giggled in Julia's arms all the way to the entrance.

After paying Vinnie's entry fee, they walked to the toddler soft play area next to the coffee shop. Sue was already there with her twins, Pearl and Dottie, who wore matching pink dresses. Sue, who had rejoined the working world now that her maternity leave was over, was in her blue nurse's uniform, ready for an evening shift at the hospital.

"Look, girls, your Auntie Julia and Uncle Vinnie are here," Sue exclaimed when she spotted them. "And your Great-Granny Dot, although by the looks of her face, we'll be calling her Grumpy-Granny Dot today."

"Did *you* know about this too?" Dot asked as she looked around, wincing at the wall of noise coming from all directions.

"I did." Sue pulled out a chair while Julia settled Vinnie in the shallow ball pit with his nieces, who were only one month younger than him. "I like it here. Reminds me that I'm not the only one crazy enough to have a baby. Don't you think you're a little overdressed?"

"What do you mean?" Dot looked down at her fur coat. "This is a *practical* item of clothing, dear."

"But the snow has stopped."

"*For now.*"

"The man on the telly said we were through

the worst of it," Sue said, arching a brow at Julia.

"Well, the papers say something different." Dot pulled her coat together. "Wait and see. I want to be ready for when the wall of snow hits. It could be any hour now. Anyway, I was *promised* lunch!"

"Sit down, and I'll get you a coffee and some cake," Sue said.

Dot sulked as she rummaged in her handbag before producing a banana. "Good job I always carry one of these around with me. Never know when you'll need one."

While Sue went to the counter to get their drinks and cakes, Julia watched the babies. She had wanted to go to the counter herself to see if Bev was working again, but for the sake of not seeming too keen, she let Sue go, although she kept her eye out for any sign of Tony's ex-wife.

When Sue returned with the drinks and cakes on a tray, Julia joined the table, leaving the kids in the capable hands of the two members of staff who were supervising the toddler play area due to it being so busy.

"So, what's the big emergency, Gran?" Sue asked as she tore off a chunk of her blueberry muffin. "It's nothing bad, is it? I wouldn't put it past you to break some terrible news over lunch."

"Considering this *isn't* lunch, you're off the hook." Dot finished her banana and neatly placed the skin on the tray. With her hands free, she rummaged in her large handbag and produced what appeared to be a scrapbook. "After Julia was almost *murdered* in cold blood—"

"I wasn't almost murdered, Gran," Julia cut in. "Let's stick to the facts."

"None of us know what *could* have happened!"

"But we know what *did* happen," Julia explained. "Did you tell Father David I fought off a machete and Shilpa that I hospitalised three of them?"

"Hardcore," Sue mumbled through her muffin.

"I may have *embellished* some details." Dot wafted her hand as though it wasn't important. "People aren't scared enough. I keep telling you girls that you never know when someone is going to jump out to kill you! Today it's your phone and rings, tomorrow it's your life!"

"You sound like Barker." Julia pulled her whistle, panic alarm, and torch out of her bag and put them on the table. "This isn't even half of it. He bought me a Swiss army knife and pepper spray!"

"That's so romantic," Dot said without a hint of sarcasm. "He really cares about you."

"Isn't pepper spray illegal?" Sue asked through another mouthful of muffin. "Where did he get his hands on that?"

"If I told you, I'd have to torch you." Julia picked up the torch and aimed it at Sue. "Don't try me. It's bright."

"I think it's good that you're prepared," Dot said as she turned the panic alarm around in her hand. "You never know what's around the corner."

"Exactly," Sue said, winking at Julia. "Today it's muggers, tomorrow it's the new ice age."

"Oh, mock all you want, dear." Dot puckered her lips before opening the thick scrapbook. "We'll see who's laughing when it happens. Let's get back to business, shall we? I asked you both here to discuss something incredibly important. After Julia's near-death experience, Percy and I decided we weren't going to sit and wait around for death to claim us, so we're speeding things up with the wedding."

"Speeding up?" Sue asked with a worried look. "Couldn't you have told me that before I stuffed my face with a muffin? I need to fit into a dress!"

"We haven't decided a date." Dot flicked through the pages. "We're still deciding on the theme."

"*Theme*?" Julia and Sue said at the same time.

"Percy wants a magic theme, but I'm thinking something Victorian."

"*Victorian?*" Julia and Sue said again.

"Yes, Victorian." Dot pursed her lips and pushed up her curls. "Is there an echo in here?" She flipped the book around and pushed it across the table. "I need your help. You've both planned weddings more recently than I have. It feels like it was one hundred years ago! I've lived so many lives since then."

"And to celebrate that, you want a Victorian wedding?" Julia asked sceptically as she flicked through the pages of elaborate costumes Dot had cut out and stuck into the book. "You were born in the 1930s."

"But look at those costumes!" Dot stabbed her finger in the book. "*Drama*! Who doesn't want a bit of excitement on their wedding day? I'm only going to get one more of them before I pop my clogs."

"Don't talk like that," Sue said. "You'll at least want to be here when we all freeze to death so you can tell us that you were right all along."

"That's true." Dot nodded, not seeming to notice the mockery. "Although, if I'm honest, I do think Percy will die before me."

"Ever the optimist." Sue glanced awkwardly at Julia as they turned the page in the book. "You're not planning on killing him off, are you?"

"Oh, no!" Dot waved both hands. "Nothing like that. Not unless he annoys me, of course. No, I just feel like my genetic makeup is superior to his. To most, actually. *Look* at me! I've just turned eighty-five, and I'm as fresh as I was thirty years ago. How many people can say they've reached my age with no major health complaints? I'm as fit as a fiddle. I think I'll just keep living."

"Well, as long as you've decided that, then I'm sure you will." Sue continued to turn the pages to look at the outfits Dot had collected, but Julia's attention drifted to the counter where she finally spotted Bev amongst the chaos.

"How do you feel about bonnets?" Dot asked, her finger tapping on her chin.

"The same way most people feel about bonnets," Sue replied under her breath. "As in, if you put a bonnet anywhere near my head, your life expectancy might not stretch out like you hope it's going to."

Dot snatched the book back and slapped it shut. She stuffed it into her bag and folded her arms like a child who had just been told they couldn't play with their favourite toy because they'd been misbehaving.

"You two are *no help* at all!" Dot snapped. "I was there to help with your wedding, Sue. And I was there for all *three* of yours, Julia! And yes, I'm counting the first one to Barker, even though you didn't actually get married. I still bought a hat, therefore, it was a wedding!"

"Thankfully it wasn't a bonnet," Sue quipped.

"Well, if that's how you're both going to be, I shall leave and go and have *a real* lunch with my *fiancé*. Julia, Sue, I hope you're happy with yourselves! I spent all night working on that book. Do you know how hard Victorian fashion magazines are to come by?"

"Not very, considering you filled the scrapbook?" Sue replied after sipping her coffee. "Sit down, Gran. We're teasing. We're happy for you! We'll help in any way we can, but just for the record, I was serious about the bonnets." Sue's eyes drifted down to the table, and they suddenly lit up as though she had just had a brilliant idea. "You've missed something so obvious!"

"An underwater wedding?"

"An *engagement party*!" Sue snapped her fingers. "You can't have a wedding before you've had an engagement party! If you really are milking this as the wedding to end all weddings, you need to hit every event, and it all starts with the engagement party."

Dot's face lit up, and Julia could practically hear the well-oiled cogs turning. Dot slowly nodded, and her finger wagged next to her head.

"Yes," she said, her nodding growing. "You're right! Why didn't I think about that? I've just had a *marvellous* idea! Girls, I need to dash. I have so much to do!"

Dot darted off. She got as far as the gate out of the toddler area before dashing back to snatch up her untouched cupcake. She stuffed it into her bag and set off at a light jog, weaving in and out of obstacles and small children. Julia pretended not to notice when she knocked over a child along the way, and from the way Sue was staring at the ceiling lights, it seemed she was too.

For the next hour, they watched the children play and talked about everything from Sue being back at work to Barker's lack of progress with his second novel. Julia was grateful that Sue danced around mentioning the mugging, most likely thanks to their lengthy phone conversation the night before. When Sue finished her second coffee, the topic of conversation switched to one Julia had been expecting earlier.

"So," Sue said with a playful smile as she mopped up crumbs from her plate with her finger, "when is it your turn?"

"You're going to have to be more specific than that."

"I'm serious, Julia." Sue flicked a crumb at her. "You and Barker are married now. It's the next step."

Julia exhaled heavily as she watched Vinnie splash amongst the plastic balls with the biggest smile anyone had ever had. "I don't know."

"Haven't you and Barker talked about it?"

"It came up in passing," Julia said with a casual shrug. "There's a lot going on right now."

"And? Do you think I was ready to get pregnant with twins? Don't believe what you read. Imagine the hardest thing you could possibly do, and then times it by two, because that's what I have. Was it Gran who said one baby felt like one and two babies felt like twenty? Well, she was right!"

"Are you trying to put me off?"

"No. I'm saying, imagine how hard it is, but going to bed every night glad that you did it." Sue looked at the twins and a smile that only came to her when she looked at her girls took over her face. "I'm always exhausted, I'm always running late, I'm always covered in something sticky or smelly, and it doesn't seem to be getting any easier, but I wouldn't change it for the world. You need to experience it. I know you have Jessie, but she came a readymade teenager. Don't you want a little baby of your own?"

"You know I do." Julia fixed on her sister with a serious gaze. "How many nights over how many years did I sob on the phone to you because Jerrad wouldn't even consider it?"

"Forget that loser!" Sue tutted. "You're with *Barker* now. Talk to him. I know he'll feel the same."

"How do you bring that up in a conversation?"

"Well, you could start with 'Barker, can you pass me the salt, and oh, by the way, do you want to have a baby with me?'" Sue looked pleased with herself. "Easy, no?"

"Easy peasy."

"So, what's stopping you?"

"What if—"

"What if *what*?" Sue reached out and rested her hand on Julia's hand. "What if he doesn't want one?"

"No." Julia shook her head as she clenched her sister's hand. "Deep down, I think he would love a baby. You should see him with Vinnie. He's amazing."

"Then what's the problem?"

"What if I've left it too late?" Julia exhaled and looked up at the ceiling. "I'm thirty-nine. I know that's hardly seen as old these days, but I'm not stupid. I know the statistics. If I'd tried in my mid-thirties, I'd have a seventy-five percent chance of getting pregnant in the first year. Do you know what that drops to when I turn forty later this year?"

"Seventy-four percent?" Sue asked with a hopeful smile.

"Fifty percent," Julia replied. "Do you know what that drops to when I turn forty-three?"

"It can't drop that much in three years," Sue said with a forced laugh. "I know I'm not a midwife, but you hear stories about women getting pregnant later and—"

"Somewhere between one and two percent," Julia cut in. "If I get to forty-three and I'm still not pregnant, there's a ninety-eight percent chance it won't happen naturally."

"There are options." Sue clenched her hand.

"IVF, adoption, surrogacy. You know I'd carry your baby in a heartbeat!"

"I know you would." Julia squeezed her hand right back. "And that's why I love you."

"How do you know all these spooky facts, anyway?"

"Late night internet searches while trapped in a loveless marriage." Julia picked up her cup and finished the last of her cold coffee. "It didn't scare me enough in my early thirties but consider me terrified now."

"Okay." Sue slapped Julia's hand three times. "You know what this means, don't you?"

"What?"

"Don't wait until you turn forty-three." Sue grinned. "Sit down with Barker and have an *honest* conversation, no matter how hard it may seem. Do you want to wake up one day at fifty resenting that you never gave it a shot? You might be more than happy enough with Barker and Jessie, but you don't want to get that far before you realise what you want."

Sue gave Julia's hand a final pat before jumping up. She pulled her coat over her nurse uniform and checked the upside-down watch clipped to her breast pocket.

"I need to get the kids back to Neil before my shift." Sue leaned in and kissed Julia on the cheek. "Talk to Barker. You've certainly given me something to think about. I turn thirty-four at the end of the month. I suppose it's time to decide if we want to turn our duo into a trio."

Sue collected Pearl and Dottie and strapped them into their giant double pram. She waved goodbye to Vinnie and headed for the door, leaving Julia to decide what to do with her Sunday afternoon.

It hadn't escaped her that it was exactly a week since the bake-off, not that she'd know it in the village. Talk had already shifted gears to Julia's unfortunate incident, and thanks to no major developments happening, or at least not happening in public, it seemed people were ready to forget that Tony Bridges had ever existed.

Julia, on the other hand, wasn't ready to let it go, despite what she'd told Barker. She'd promised him she wouldn't put herself in danger by investigating, and she didn't intend to. There was nothing dangerous about visiting Bev's place of work to try to talk to her again.

Julia lingered around for another hour, hoping that Bev would eventually give in to her vice. When the coffee shop finally quieted down, Bev grabbed her jacket and headed for the front door. Julia scooped up Vinnie and followed behind.

"Oh, it's you again," Bev said as she lit a cigarette. "Stand on my other side. You'll be upwind from me."

Julia did as she was told and watched as Bev's cigarette smoke drifted in the opposite direction of them. Julia took another cautionary step back and put Vinnie over her shoulder, not that Bev seemed to mind.

"Did you hear about that woman who got mugged in Fern Moore the other night?" Bev mumbled through her cigarette. "It was the same night we were on the bus. Did you see anything?"

"No," Julia lied, not in the mood to recount the tale again. "I heard about it though. I heard she's fine."

"Hmm." Bev sucked hard on her cigarette. "I'm not sure you'd ever be fine again after something like that. Not really."

Julia cleared her throat. She had to bite her tongue, she so desperately wanted to tell Bev she was strong enough to not let a single moment define her life.

"How are you doing, Bev?"

"Police dragged me in again yesterday." She stated in a matter-of-fact voice. "Claimed they had new evidence, but it was nothing. They're chasing their own tails trying to pin this on me."

"What new evidence?"

"Just some old pictures from a bad period in my life." Bev's thin lips curled around her cigarette as her eyes fogged over. "It's nothing. It wasn't relevant, and they knew it. I left when I realised I wasn't under arrest."

Balancing Vinnie on her hip, Julia pulled a pile of printed out photographs from her bag and handed them to Bev. She tossed her cigarette on the floor and stamped it out before flicking through the images.

"Where did you get these?" Bev asked coolly.

"They were on Tony's assistant's laptop."

"And you're carrying them around in your bag because...?"

"I wanted to see how you'd react when I showed them to you." Julia took the pictures back and tucked them away. "As it happens, it seems like a waste of my printer's ink because you didn't react at all. Consider me a little embarrassed."

"I'm not going to lie about my past." Bev checked her watch. "I only have a couple more minutes before they come looking for me. Why are you so interested in me? I don't think it's a coincidence that you're here again. The first time I could believe, but you came here today for a reason."

Julia considered her thoughts for a moment. Whatever she chose to say next could make the difference between Bev opening up and giving her more useful information, or Bev running off and never speaking to Julia again.

"I have a keen interest in local crime," Julia admitted. "Although, saying that out loud makes me sound a little peculiar."

"Just a bit."

"I just want to know what happened to Tony," Julia said, dropping her guard. "We were both there. We both saw it. Why would someone kill him that way? They could have slipped peanuts to him any time. Why there?"

"And why my cake?" Bev huffed and leaned against the metal exterior of the building. "I could have been chosen at random, but out of all those people, it just happened to be the ex-wife? No wonder that DI is salivating at the thought of charging me. It's a picture-perfect ending."

"Why did you enter the bake-off?"

"What do you mean?"

"You don't live in Peridale." Julia stepped closer now that Bev had stopped smoking. "They're holding them all over the county. If you really love baking, which I think you do because your red velvet was near perfect, you could have entered any of them, but you chose to enter the one your ex-husband happened to be judging."

"Is there anything wrong with wanting to rub it in your ex-husband's face?" Bev asked. "Don't act like you wouldn't show off your ring and talk about how happy you were if your ex showed up out of the blue. I had nothing to show off, other than that I'd let him go. The woman in those pictures was sick. I don't deny how difficult I found the divorce. Wouldn't anyone? After nearly twenty years of marriage, he threw me out onto the street without a penny to my name. He moved Camila in the next day. I wasn't standing outside *their* house, I was standing outside *my* house. Tony might have paid for it, but who do you think made that house a home while he was at work? I was angry, and I wanted them to know it. I put my life into that place, and I got nothing in return. I tried so hard to get Tony back. I tried *too* hard for *too* long. I didn't realise what I was doing half the time. Looking back now, I know I acted crazy, but at the time, I thought I was doing it out of love. When I finally stepped back and let them get on with their lives, I found some peace. That's why I went to the bake-off. I wanted to show him that he didn't affect me anymore."

Bev paused and scrambled for another cigarette with trembling hands.

"Look at me, I'm back smoking, and I'm working in the noisiest place on the planet. Tony and I might never have had kids, but it didn't mean I didn't desperately want them. After what happened with Judy, he didn't want to go through that again. Now I have to spend my days surrounded by them, and I hate to burst the bubble, but it's not fun when they're not your own. I go home, and my back is killing me, my ears are ringing, and it takes a full bottle of wine before I even feel human. And now the cigarettes are back! I should be living the best years of my life right now, but these are truly the worst."

"They could be worse."

"How?"

"You could have still been married to Tony." Julia offered her a playful smile. "I know we don't know each other, but your life doesn't have to end because of this. My gran is eighty-five and has just got engaged."

"*Eighty-five?*" Bev choked on her smoke. "Wow. I don't think I'll still be around then if I carry on like this."

"Tomorrow's a new day." Julia glanced at her watch; she'd taken up more than enough of Bev's smoke break. "Just one more thing before you go back. I have some more pictures. Tony thought he was being followed, and it seems he was right. Do you have any idea who this man is?"

Julia passed her the second lot of pictures from her bag. Bev flicked through a couple, but she shook her head.

"No idea. Sorry. That could be anyone." Bev stamped out her second cigarette and blew out the smoke. "I need to get back now. If you ever want to stop treating me like a suspect, we could be friends. I heard you're a good baker, but I'm not too bad myself. See you around."

Julia carried Vinnie to the car. He had fallen asleep somewhere during the conversation, which didn't surprise her, given he was late for his afternoon nap and had been playing at full speed for hours. She buckled him carefully into the car seat, which Barker had kindly transferred over to her car, and set off back to Peridale, this time without a detour through Fern Moore.

Could Julia trust Bev? Despite having so much in common, from their messy divorces to their love of baking, a nagging voice in the back of her head told her to keep her distance.

12

"So, you talked to Oliver?" Johnny urged on Julia's doorstep early on Monday morning. "What did he tell you?"

"Tony was being followed by a man." Julia handed over the pictures she'd printed off. "That's all I got from him. Well, that's all I think is important. And no, before you ask, I haven't figured out who he is."

"Yet."

"I'm glad you have faith, Johnny." Julia pulled her dressing gown close as a chilly wind whipped down the lane. "I don't have much to work on."

"Have you talked to the wife yet?"

"Briefly."

"And?"

"She was understandably grief-stricken, and I didn't want to push too hard." Julia shivered as the cold air sucked all the heat from her cottage. "Are you coming in? I spent all morning heating this place, and I have a baby in here."

"I can't stay." Johnny glanced at his girlfriend's cottage across the lane. "Leah has given me a key, and I'm going to let myself in and surprise her with breakfast in bed. Do you think she'll like that?"

"Just don't make it a total surprise. The sun has barely shown its face. You might give her the fright of her life."

"I never thought of that." He fiddled with his glasses. "I'll just have to be extra quiet. Keep me in the loop!"

Leaving Johnny to hopefully surprise and not shock Leah, Julia retreated to her cereal and cup of tea in the kitchen. Her corn flakes had turned to mush, but the cold had blown her appetite away. Barker helped Vinnie with his own breakfast, watching her as she scraped the mess into the bin.

"Your phone beeped when you were at the

door." Barker nodded to her phone on the counter. "What did Johnny want?"

"Gossip for the paper." Julia picked up her phone. "What does he ever want? Oh, it's from my dad. He says Katie is recovering well, but they still haven't cleared her to fly."

"It's been *eight* days." Barker huffed as he spooned more cereal into Vinnie's open mouth. "How much longer do you think they'll be?"

"As long as it takes. She has pins in her legs and can barely stand up straight without three people helping her." Julia cocked her head and watched as Barker matched Vinnie's facial expressions. "It's not a problem, is it?"

"No," Barker said, his tone unsure. "It would just be nice to get back to normal. Don't get me wrong, I love having Vinnie around, but you have to admit it's a lot of work."

"Babies are." Julia turned around, looking through the kitchen window to hide her face from Barker. Emotion swept over her in an instant. Since her frank conversation with Sue the day before, the words had been on the tip of her tongue. They were desperate to fall out, to fill the silence with a question so huge it would change everything in an instant. She parted her lips, and her throat even grunted, but the words wouldn't come.

"Do you … do you … do you want another coffee?"

"I'd love another coffee." Barker leaned over and kissed her on the cheek. "That's why we're so perfect for each other. We can practically read each other's minds."

Julia stared deep into his eyes. She desperately willed him to read exactly what was on her mind so she didn't have to be the one to bring it up.

"Are you feeling okay? Your eyes are shiny."

"Allergies," Julia said, turning away to wipe a fallen tear.

It almost hurt that he didn't question her further since, unlike Tony Bridges, she didn't have any allergies.

***

Once again, Jessie insisted that she run the café on her own and that Julia stay home with Vinnie. Julia knew Jessie didn't want a rambunctious toddler running around the café on a quiet Monday, which Jessie would likely spend consumed by her phone—not that Julia minded. It gave her a chance to cross another person off her list without throwing herself into a dangerous situation.

"I'm going to take Vinnie for a walk," she called to Barker, who was too deep in his writing to question her. "I won't be too long."

As Julia pushed Vinnie's pram up the winding lane in the direction of Peridale Farm, she felt the first hint that spring would soon take over the village. The afternoon air still held a chill, but the snow had completely melted. For the first time in a full week, the sky wasn't masked with a sheet of hazy clouds. Staring up at the pure blue sky, she vowed never to take it for granted again.

They bypassed the farm, taking a narrow lane that ran alongside it instead. More than once, she had to push herself into the bushes to allow cars up and down. She was using her memory of a map she had seen that morning to lead her in the general direction, not that she needed it by the time she reached the bottom of the lane. The scent of horse manure was so thick in the air, it pulled her in the right direction.

The Peridale Riding Centre was so tucked away deep in the countryside, it was easy to forget the place was even there. Julia hadn't given it much thought since her sole visit in her early teens when

Sue had been deep in her horse-riding phase. She'd somehow convinced Julia, who would've rather been at home baking, to give it a try, and with Dot's encouragement and the help of a stepping stool, Julia had mounted a small chestnut pony. Unlike Sue, who possessed the natural elegance and poise needed to ride, Julia was awkward and clumsy on the back of the animal. She panicked, kicked too hard, spooked the horse, and was ejected from her saddle and into the dust within thirty seconds. The bruise on her backside was enough to put her off ever wanting to try again, and even though the instructors had tried to convince her to 'get back on the horse', Julia had sat on a grooming box, embarrassed and sore, where she remained until Sue had finished and they could leave.

When the riding school finally came into view, Julia didn't recognise it as the place she had visited as a child. She remembered a single row of stables with a mucky outdoor riding ring, but a lot had changed in the almost three decades since. The row of stables she remembered was still there, but it paled in comparison to the giant structure that had been built to house the indoor stables. A larger outdoor school had also been built, and there was even an indoor school for when the weather wasn't as good.

Even though Julia hadn't given the place much thought since her childhood, it appeared enough people cared, because even on a quiet Monday, it was teaming with life. Children of all ages ran around in their tight jodhpurs, dirty riding boots, thick hoodies, and riding hats. They were leading horses, brushing and washing them, mucking out, feeding, riding, and, despite there still being a chill in the air, they all looked like they wouldn't want to be doing anything else after a long day of school.

Feeling like the fraud she was, Julia approached with trepidation. She let herself in via a large metal gate and pushed Vinnie into the concrete yard in front of the indoor stables. To the left of the stables, she immediately spotted Florence Henshaw, the feisty redhead who had thrown the coffee in Tony's face an hour before his death. She stood in the middle of the outdoor school, surrounded by four small children atop ponies listening while she barked her instructions.

"C'mon, Ella!" she cried, her authoritative tone cutting through the air. "You're supposed to be doing a rising trot! I want to see your bottom actually *rising* from the saddle. *That's it*! Keep your back straight!"

Remembering what she'd once been told about never walking directly behind a horse, Julia walked around the edge of the yard to the gate of the school, where parents stood watching their kids during their lesson.

"Okay, everyone, we're going to do a little sequence to finish off, okay?" Florence said before clapping her hands together. "Remember what I told you last week about X? Where is X?"

"In the middle," the four children chorused.

"That's right." Florence looked pleased with herself. "Right where I am standing. Now, taking turns and not getting too close to each other, I want you to go from A, to B, to C, to E, and then finish at X in a neat line. Can you do that?"

"Yeah," they called.

Florence ran over to the gate and leaned against it while the children performed what she had asked of them. They headed one by one to the letters tacked to the outskirts of the fence, and then to the middle. The children looked around seven, but none of them struggled with the task. Julia could feel the embarrassment from her fall regurgitating itself through the decades.

"*Perfect*!" Florence called out. "Now, do I need to go and get the step, or can you all dismount on your own?"

The four children all dismounted with no trouble at once. Once again, Florence looked pleased with herself.

"Excellent." Florence swung open the gate and shooed the parents away. "What do we say about the step?"

"*Steps are for first-time riders, and never again,*" they chanted.

Despite Florence's somewhat dictatorial approach to her teaching, the parents were all brimming with proud smiles. The children seemed disciplined, able to take instruction, and well-behaved for such a young age. Maybe Julia had missed out on something after all?

The four children led the ponies into the indoor stable, leaving the parents to linger by their cars, most of which were giant SUVs and sports cars. Julia remembered the price list on the website; riding certainly wasn't an affordable hobby to take up. When the school was empty, Florence shut the gate and marched right past Julia without giving her a second glance. She got the impression Florence was there because she loved horses and teaching, and she was less interested in the parents who tagged along to watch, not that

Julia was one of those parents.

Julia followed Florence into the indoor stables and watched as she ducked into a dimly lit office, which was cluttered with children sizing their hats. Florence filtered through them and consulted a large book on the desk before checking her watch. She drank from a bottle of what appeared to be an energy drink before emerging ready for whatever was next on the schedule. Not wanting to miss her opportunity, Julia pushed Vinnie forward and blocked Florence's path.

"Hello there," Julia said as sweetly as she could. "I was wondering if you could help me?"

"What is it?" Florence stood with her feet wide apart and her hands on her hips on the inside of her quilted jacket. "The baby is too young for lessons, although if you come back in a year, I have a tiny pony I can throw him on."

Florence went to step around Julia, but she countered, using the pram as a blockade. Florence stared Julia dead in the eyes, and it was obvious she wasn't used to people being so forceful on her premises.

"I used to ride here as a little girl," Julia started, trying to summon as much of Sue as she could. "It's changed a lot since, but I still remember it fondly. I adored it, you see, and I've wanted to throw myself back into it for years, but I never had the courage, so I thought I'd come and talk to you about possibly booking some lessons?"

"Oh, you're one of *those.*" Florence rolled her eyes. "You don't *talk* about horse riding, you *do* it. How you remember prancing around on a pony as a little girl will bear little resemblance to what it's like learning to ride as an adult."

"Yes, I understand that, but—"

"*Josh!*" she yelled down the row of stables. "Bring out Samson. He's already tacked up and ready to go."

Florence tilted her head and assessed Julia with a level of scrutiny that made Julia feel like her personal space was being invaded.

"You have quite a large head," Florence stated. "*Luke?* Bring me a seven and a quarter hat. Actually, make that the seven and three-eighths."

Before Julia knew what was happening, a large riding hat was being crammed on her head and fastened under her chin. It dropped forward, covering her eyes. She pushed it back to see that Vinnie had been wheeled away by a group of teenage girls, and a red step had been placed in front of her. Samson, as it turned out, was a black horse so large, Julia had to crane her neck to look up at him.

"I—I—I—"

"Isn't he a beauty?" Florence slapped his neck as she kicked the step towards him. "Eighteen hands from foot to shoulder. That's six foot in normal speak. More if you count his head." Florence admired the horse for a moment before turning to Julia with a wicked grin. "Well, what are you waiting for? Climb on up. You said you wanted to get back into riding."

Julia felt the colour drain from her face as she looked helplessly around the stable. All eyes were on her, and they all shared a similar grin that let her know she was taking part in a frequent ritual of public humiliation.

"No?" Florence said. "Are you sure?"

Julia gulped, and for a moment, she actually considered climbing atop the horse to prove some vague point. As though her inner child was screaming out, her bottom suddenly hurt, and she imagined how much more painful it would be to fall as a thirty-nine-year-old from a horse taller than any human she'd ever met.

"I think there's been a misunderstanding," Julia said, forcing the shake from her voice as she stepped away from the horse. "I—I—I just—"

"Relax, love." Florence knocked on Julia's hat. "I'm pulling your leg. It's a little game we like to play around here to see how far people get. For a second, I actually thought you were going to do it. Even I need a stiff drink before braving this beast."

The teenager who'd brought the horse led it back to its stable, and the hat and step disappeared as quickly as they'd appeared. Vinnie was returned to Julia with a carton of juice that one of the girls must have given him.

"You should have seen the look on your face." Florence chuckled. "Picture perfect."

"Yes, very funny." Julia tried to laugh, but her nerves were too shaken.

"Listen, let's stop the games." Florence lowered her voice and turned serious for the first time. "I know why you're here. I saw you at the bake-off when I gave Tony a taste of his own medicine. They warned me you might show up."

"They?"

"The police." Florence motioned for Julia to join her in the office. "Leave the baby. He'll be looked after. Couldn't find a better group of kids if you tried."

Trusting her word, Julia left Vinnie with the

girls, who seemed more than happy to fuss over him. Following Florence, Julia cast her gaze up the row of stables to the giant horse at the bottom who had extra high walls compared to the other horses. In the split-second before she looked away, she saw someone who looked strangely familiar walking out of one of the stables with a wheelbarrow.

"I could have sworn I just saw Tony's wife."

"Camila?" Florence replied as she shut the door behind Julia. "Yeah, she keeps her horse here, although I'm not sure for how much longer. She's a month behind on livery. I'll let her off this once because her husband just died, but I'm not running a charity." Florence sat behind the tiny desk and motioned for Julia to sit across from her. The small office's walls were made from exposed cinderblocks and were covered in years of cobwebs mixed with dust and hay. An overwhelming number of tatty and well-used hats lined one of the walls on shelves that looked ready to snap under the sheer weight of them. The desk was just as dusty, with an open book for lessons sat on top a mountain of paperwork.

"Help yourself to mints." Florence motioned to the stacks of boxes behind Julia's chair. "They're a couple of months out of date, but we get them cheap because the horses love them."

Julia declined the offer, but Florence reached past her and grabbed a tube. She peeled back the foil and popped the circular discs into her mouth one by one.

"So, does this mean I'm a suspect in your little mystery?" Florence said while crunching the mints. "How exciting! I don't make my way into the village all that often. I'm much more suited out here. I get my shopping delivered, and I have all the company I'll ever want. This place is full morning till night. I suppose you want to know why I threw coffee in the *beloved* Tony Bridges' face?"

"I would."

"I hope you haven't lost any sleep over it." Florence finished the packet of mints and tossed the wrapper into an overflowing bin. "I didn't kill him, but you don't think that, do you? You would have been here sooner if you *actually* thought I'd killed him. I *wish* I had. Peanut oil in the cake? *Genius*! It's a good job I love my horses too much, or I would have done much worse to that awful man."

"The coffee?"

"He killed one of my horses," Florence said

bluntly. "Turned up to collect Camila three weeks ago, and he reversed right into Rocky. A beautiful chestnut Shetland. Broke two of his legs, and—you know what we do to horses with broken legs?"

Julia nodded, gulping hard.

"Then I won't go into the gory details." Florence cleared her throat, and she seemed to be holding back tears. "Reversing into Rocky? I could *almost* forgive that. I won't pretend like this is the most organised operation in the land. There's always kids and horses cluttering the place, and accidents do happen." Florence's jaw gritted tightly. "Tony driving off like nothing had happened? Again, I could *almost* forgive that. He was driving a big Range Rover. Maybe he didn't realise what he'd done? What decent human being would hit a horse and then *knowingly* leave without trying to see what happened?"

"No one would do that."

"Exactly. As you probably found out for yourself, Tony Bridges was the furthest thing from a decent man. I listened to his radio show here and there. I never developed much of an opinion on him, but I didn't dislike him. Then, Camila moved her horse here, and though Tony would come to pick her up, he never got out to talk to anyone. I never held it against him. I thought it might have been nice for him to say hello to the kids, being a local celebrity, but I wasn't in denial. These places aren't for everyone. The smell alone is enough to make you run."

"You get used to it."

"Don't lie." Florence half-smiled. "Horses stink. I love them, but they do. I've always loved horses more than people, but that doesn't mean I hate people, I just find horses uncomplicated in comparison. I can honestly say I didn't hate anyone until I chased that man's Range Rover to the top of the lane. Again, I thought maybe he couldn't see me, or maybe he had the radio turned on so he couldn't hear me shouting after him. When his eyes met mine in the side mirror, I realised he was ignoring me on purpose, and knew very well what he'd done. Can you guess what he did next?"

"Got out and apologised?"

"He sped up." Florence leaned forward across the table, her eyes inches from Julia's. "That man looked me in the eye, knowing he'd just killed one of my horses, and he sped up. If that's not pure evil, I don't know what is." The red mist faded. "I didn't stop running until he had to stop for a tractor up near the farm. The man wouldn't even roll down his window for me. Camila, bless her, realised what I was screaming about, and she got out, but Tony sped off the second the tractor moved. The only reason Camila is still on this yard right now is because she walked me back here, holding me together. I couldn't see through the tears. She was the last person to leave that night. I will never understand why she was married to that man."

"I don't know what to say."

"There's nothing to say." Florence sighed. "After the shock wore off, I got my lawyers involved. Camila kept apologising on his behalf, but it wasn't enough. I couldn't undo what he did, but I could certainly rinse him for every penny. And then the idiot had to go and die, which I suppose is better revenge." She stood and consulted the book again. "I'm already five minutes late for my teens' group lesson, and teenagers aren't known for their patience. I hope I've helped in some way."

"You have," Julia said. "At least I know you didn't do it."

"You believe me?"

"Why wouldn't I?"

Florence smiled as she opened the door for Julia.

"I like you, lady." Florence shook Julia's hand as she walked out. "If you actually want to get back into riding, you know where we are."

Florence headed back to the school where the next group were already waiting on their horses. Julia retrieved Vinnie and thanked the girls for looking after him. Before she left, she circled the entire riding centre, making sure to check every stable, but Camila was nowhere to be seen. Julia wondered if she was hiding, or if she had been on her way home when Julia saw her. Either way, she had missed an opportunity to speak with the elusive widow.

As Julia walked back up the steep lane, she cast her mind to one man who had probably spoken to Camila on more than one occasion. She pulled her phone from her bag and scrolled to one of her least-used contacts.

"Hello, it's Julia. I wanted to talk to you about the case. Can we meet? The Plough at five? I'll see you there."

13

With Vinnie back at the cottage with Barker, Julia indulged in a glass of white wine while she waited for DI John Christie to show his face at The Plough. She hadn't expected him to be early, but when he arrived forty minutes late, she had almost given up on him.

"Do you mind if I get a pint?" he asked when he arrived, with no apology or explanation for his lateness. "I need it. Do you want a refill?"

Julia nodded as she drained her glass. She hadn't intended on drinking more than one, but if a little alcohol loosened Christie's tongue, she didn't mind joining in. When he returned with their drinks, he planted himself in the seat opposite her and pulled off his tie; he looked drained.

"Rough day?" she asked after sipping her wine.

"You could say that." Christie gulped down a quarter of his pint and wiped his mouth with the back of his hand. "On top of getting nowhere with the Bridges' case, a car was stolen from a guest staying at the B&B. Guess where it turned up on fire?"

"Fern Moore?"

"Bingo." Christie chuckled darkly. "It was burning in the middle of the place, and no one called the police. They're all too used to looking the other way. Can you imagine that happening in the village? The station phone would be ringing before they'd finished dousing the thing in petrol."

"Any idea who took it?"

"Wouldn't be surprised if it was the same lads who mugged you." Christie took another sip of beer. "If you've asked me here about that, I'm afraid I don't have anything for you. Bus company claims their cameras weren't working that day, and they don't know who was driving the bus because the systems were somehow wiped. I think they're trying to protect the driver."

"Why?"

"Because I checked the timetable, and it wasn't the end of the line." Christie unbuttoned his collar and sighed heavily. "He kicked you off because he couldn't be bothered driving you to the next stop ten minutes down the road. If they give him up, he could be liable for what happened to you."

Julia sipped her wine, unsure what to think about the driver who had thrown her off the bus. He hadn't seemed like the friendliest man, but he wasn't to blame for what had happened to her. What's to say she wouldn't have driven herself to Fern Moore after reading Johnny's text?

"Don't go looking for him," Julia said. "It's not his fault. What about the kids who actually did it?"

"Oh, I know who they all are." Christie leaned into his chair and rested his hands behind his head, showing the sweat stains under his arms. "Figured that out within the day. I have a few informants over there who are willing to squeal to protect themselves. The problem is, I can't prove anything. Unless they're caught red-handed trying to get rid of the jewellery they stole, there's nothing I can do. They had their faces covered, you won't be able to identify them confidently, and they'll all lie through their teeth claiming to be each other's alibis. Nothing would stand up in court, and they know that. Why do you think they do it in the first place? The estate should be bulldozed to the ground, with or without those scumbags inside."

"They're still human beings, Christie."

"*Hardly*!"

"They're kids who haven't had the best upbringing. They could still turn their lives around."

"And do you think they're going to?" Christie glared at Julia. "Even with all the will in the world, people like that won't change because they don't want to. Crime pays, Julia, especially when you can get away with it. The odd few might get out, but most of the people who are born there never leave, and if they do, it's usually to spend some time behind bars, which sounds like a holiday compared to living there. I can't believe you'd even defend that place after what they did to you."

Julia silently sipped her wine, not wanting to cause a full-blown row with DI Christie. Despite how some residents of the estate acted, she knew they weren't all lost causes. People like Oliver and Addie proved that. She suspected that, at the end of the day, a lot of the people behind those flat doors were decent; their reputations tarnished by a vocal few. No matter what Christie thought, she hadn't invited him there to talk about her mugging, and she didn't want him to storm out.

"I guess there's been no sign of my rings or the locket?"

"Not a peep." He gave her a sympathetic smile. "When I say I'm trying to find them, I really mean it. I know how much that pearl ring means to you. Even if I can't lock those kids up, I promise I won't stop looking for your jewellery."

Julia was touched by Christie's determination. She hadn't expected his edges to soften towards her, but if that was the one thing to come out of the mugging, she would take it. She waited until he had drained his first pint and ordered a second before getting to what she really wanted to talk about.

"Still think Bev killed Tony?" she asked, running her finger around the rim of her glass.

"Don't you?"

"I have my doubts."

"Why?" Christie wiped beer foam from his top lip. "She was caught red-handed."

"And yet she's not been charged."

"Because the woman is *sneaky*!" Christie stamped his finger on the table. "She's calling our bluff. She poisoned that cake knowing it would look like a set-up, and that she'd come out looking the victim."

"What if she is?"

"I don't trust her face." Christie pushed the tip of his nose up. "If you know what I mean."

"That's just cruel!" Julia tossed a beer mat at him. "She seems all right to me. I've had two conversations with her, and she doesn't strike me as the murderous type."

"Oh, and she must be innocent because Julia South thinks so?"

"Julia South-*Brown*," Julia corrected him. "Married, remember?"

"Then where's the ring to prove it?" Christie tossed back the beer mat with a deep belly laugh. "Oh, Julia. Barker is lucky to have you."

Julia was taken about by his sudden playful side—something she had never seen. She hid her face behind her wine glass after taking a deep drink.

"Why's that?"

"Because you *care*," Christie cried. "And not

just about Barker. You care about anything and everything. Do you know what my wife cares about?" Christie waited for Julia to respond. She simply shrugged. "Me neither! She sits in front of that telly all day, eating crisps and watching shows about housewives from all over America. She doesn't even look at me when I come home."

"I'm sure she cares."

"You think?" Christie tossed back more beer. "We don't even sleep in the same room. I've been in the guest bedroom since Christmas." He paused. "I don't know why I'm telling you this."

Julia didn't either. She was more than a little shocked that the DI was being so open with her. She put it down to the beer, but he hadn't drunk enough for him to start spilling his deepest secrets without realising what he was saying.

"Christie, I—"

"Ignore me." He sat up straight and cleared his throat. "It's just been a long day. I haven't slept properly in days. Weeks, even. If it's not one thing keeping me up, it's another."

"Do you not have anyone to talk to?"

His eyes met hers, and for a moment, she thought he was going to put up a wall so high she'd never be able to ask about the case, but he shook his head, and his posture relaxed.

"Barker's my only real friend," Christie admitted. "And how do you talk about this stuff to other men? The boys at the station are fine, but I'm their superior. It's not the same as when I was under Barker."

"Barker would be there for you if you needed him to be."

"He's too busy being a best-selling author to care about my marriage troubles." Christie laughed as he stared into his pint. "He's living *the* life."

"It's not so easy for him right now, you know," she revealed, immediately wondering if she should have said anything. "He's having trouble with his publishers. They're not liking his second book."

"Really?"

"Maybe you could talk to each other?" she suggested. "There's no shame in talking about your emotions."

"Yeah, maybe." Christie stared into his pint for a second before clearing his throat and leaning against the table. "So, why did you really ask me here? I'm sure it wasn't to hear me moan about my wife, and I doubt it's about your mugging, either."

Sensing that he was ready to give her what she

wanted to know, Julia pulled the folded pictures from her handbag. She opened them and placed them on the table. Christie cast his eye over them, and it became obvious straight away that he'd seen them before.

"Where did you get these?" Christie asked with a crooked smile; Julia could tell he was impressed. "Are you sure you don't want to retrain? It's never too late. I'd kill for a brain like yours on my team."

"I'm flattered, but no." Julia pushed the pictures closer. "I assume you've seen these? Tony thought he was being followed by this man."

"He *was* being followed by this man." Christie paused to sip his pint. "Nigel Bell."

"You know him?"

"Very well." Christie leaned across the table and pushed the pictures back to Julia. "Our paths have crossed quite a few times over the years. He's a PI. A private investigator. Well, not officially. He's not registered."

"You have to be registered to be a PI?"

"Since 2014." Christie nodded. "They thought it would put a stop to the unscrupulous PIs out there, but they're still working. Nigel Bell is a decent. He's not one of the bad ones, but they'd never officially register him and he knows it, so he operates on the outskirts. If he caused trouble, we'd be able to give him six months of jail time and a hefty fine, but he can be useful from time to time."

"Why was he following Tony?"

"Nigel specialises in cheating spouses," Christie said with a twinkle in his eye. "He follows men around when their wives think they're being naughty. It's simple stuff. Men aren't that careful about these things, usually. We're an arrogant breed. We think we're never going to get caught, but when do cheaters ever get away with it?"

"Camila hired him?"

"That's my guess," Christie said after more beer. "She won't admit it. I asked her, and she swore she'd never do that. Claimed to trust him, which I thought was sweet. If we hadn't been in the middle of an official interview, I would have told her never to trust a man."

"I trust Barker."

"Barker's different." Christie pursed his lips. "I don't think he'd have it in him. The soppy bugger only has eyes for you. Tony, on the other hand, was quite the adulterer, or so I heard. Cheated on his first wife with Bev, and then on Bev with Camila. I think Camila was trying to find out who her replacement was before he shocked her with divorce papers."

"And did Nigel find anything?"

"He wouldn't tell me. Client confidentiality, or so he claims. He wouldn't confirm or deny Camila was the one who'd hired him, but it was obviously her, wasn't it?"

"Seems like it." Julia picked up her wine and sat back in her chair as her mind worked. "Do you know where Camila lives?"

"I do, but I'm not telling you." Christie finished his pint and grabbed his tie off the table. "I need to get back home, not that the wife will even notice I'm not there yet. Thanks for the pints, by the way. I started a tab under your name." Christie winked. "Try not to get yourself killed, and if you tell anyone that I told you any of this stuff, I'll deny this conversation ever happened."

After settling the bill, Julia left the pub to walk home. She only took five steps before her phone rang.

"*Julia?*" Dot cried down the handset. "Where are you?"

"Walking home from the pub."

"The Plough? *Great*! Come to my cottage *right now*! It's *important*!"

"Gran, I—"

"Important, Julia! Your sister is already here."

Before Julia could say anything else, Dot hung up. Knowing nothing good would come from trying to argue with her gran, Julia walked to her cottage. She noticed that her café lights were still on, but she put it down to Jessie taking her time cleaning after close.

"Where's the fire?" Julia called as she let herself into her gran's cottage. "Barker is expecting me back..."

Julia clasped her hand over her mouth when she walked into her gran's sitting room. She tried to hold back the laughter, but the two glasses of wine made it impossible to keep it in.

"Shut up," Sue cried. "Just shut up!"

"You look..."

"I said *shut up!*"

But Julia couldn't stop laughing. She looked Sue up and down, unsure what she was dressed as, but enjoying it all the same. A dark maroon velvet gown suffocated her from her neck to her wrists and down to her toes. A matching velvet hat with a plume of feathers jutting out, almost scraping the exposed beams in the ceiling, balanced on her head. Her waist had been nipped in with what appeared to be a corset, and she held a frilly umbrella in one hand and a large fan in the other. The transformation didn't end at the costume either. Her face had been powdered white, and her cheeks were bright red.

Unable to stop herself, Julia pulled her phone out of her pocket and opened the camera. She snapped a handful of pictures before Sue whacked her with the umbrella.

"The camera on this new phone is excellent." Julia chuckled as she looked through the pictures. "It really captures your joy. What does Neil think of your new look?"

"*Neil*?" Sue cried, stumbling forward but hardly able to move under the restrictive layers. "Neil will *never* see this! No one will!"

"He'll see you at the party!" Dot appeared behind Julia, dressed in a matching emerald green outfit. "This was your idea, Sue."

"*Was it*?" Sue cried, collapsing stiffly into the armchair. "I don't remember asking for this!"

"An engagement party was a *wonderful* idea." Dot cracked open her fan and wafted her face, her other hand resting on her stomach. "I can barely breathe, but don't I look wonderful? I think I might start dressing like this every day."

Dot fiddled with her signature brooch, which

she had pinned to the high, frilly collar of her dress.

"You do look rather fetching, Dorothy," Percy said as he appeared behind her. "I could get used to this."

Percy was similarly dressed in a purple velvet tuxedo, with a penguin coat so long the tails touched the floor. A monocle, top hat, and cane completed the look, and he'd even gone to the trouble of sticking on a fake twirled moustache.

"Your costume is waiting for you in the dining room, Julia," Dot announced. "Go and try it on. We need to make sure it fits. The engagement party is tomorrow night."

"*Tomorrow?*"

"The village hall is booked, the invitations went out this morning, and Jessie made one of those internet event thingies just to be sure!"

"Not laughing now, are you, big sis?" Sue smirked as she fanned herself. "I can't wait to see you in yours."

After reluctantly changing into her costume in the dining room, Julia assessed her black and white outfit in the reflection of the dark window. Feeling like she had somehow drawn the short straw, Julia waddled into the sitting room, barely able to breathe in the tight corset.

"What did I do to upset you, Gran?" Julia asked as she brushed down the white apron over her black dress. "I'm a *maid*? *Seriously*?"

"Nice bonnet," Sue said with a thumbs up. "Really suits you."

"Look at you!" Dot clapped her hands together. "Oh, this is going to be amazing! People are going to talk about this for decades. It was such a good idea to use this theme for the engagement party. I've had an *even* better idea for the wedding!"

"Shakespearean dress?" Sue mocked.

"No," Dot said with a wave of her fan before tensing her brows. "Although, that's not a bad idea! Oh, isn't this fun? Why did we ever stop dressing like this?"

"Because it's uncomfortable!" Julia cried as she struggled for breath. "I'm not wearing this! Why does Sue get to be a lady and I'm stuck being the maid?"

"Someone needs to be the maid, dear," Dot said as she fussed with Julia's curls. "And this was all they had in your size. I think your hair should be up for the party. It's more in keeping with the style. What do you think, Percy?"

"Oh, yes." Percy nodded, squinting through his monocle. "You have such an eye for detail,

Dorothy."

"I know, dear." Dot fluffed up her curls. "Julia, make us all some tea, will you?"

"Are you being serious right—"

"Oi, maids don't talk back!" Sue poked Julia in the corseted stomach with the butt of her umbrella. "Make mine a green tea, will you? There's a good girl."

Barely able to comprehend what was happening, Julia retreated into the kitchen and filled the kettle. While it boiled, she stared at her reflection in the microwave door, wondering how she'd gone from having a serious conversation with a DI in the pub to being dressed as a Victorian maid and making tea in her gran's kitchen.

"Don't question it, Julia," she whispered. "You'll drive yourself insane."

Ignoring Sue's request for green tea, Julia crammed a handful of tea bags into a teapot before filling it with boiling water. She grabbed four cups and carried them into the sitting room on a tray. Sue was waiting with her phone to take revenge pictures of Julia; she should have expected it.

"The tray just completes the look." Sue chuckled as she slotted her phone into the top of her outfit. "I think you should carry it around with you tomorrow."

"That's a good idea!" Dot called from her position at the window. "Oh, you'll do the food for us, won't you? We haven't hired anyone."

"Gran…" Julia sighed. "What do you expect me to pull together in a night?"

"You'll think of something!" Dot muttered as she pushed her nose close to the window.

"What are you doing?" Julia asked as she struggled to bend over to set the tray on the table.

"Spying." Dot turned around to show her tiny binoculars on a long stick. "There's someone in your café."

"Did those come with your costume?"

"No. I've had them for months."

Julia walked over to the window and pulled back the net curtains to look at what Dot was seeing. She took the binoculars and squinted through them at her brightly lit café across the dark village green. As clear as day, she saw Jessie sitting across the table from a man.

"That's *him*!" Dot said, snatching the binoculars off Julia. "That's *the man*!"

"What man?" Sue called.

"The man from Mulberry Lane!" Dot passed the binoculars to Percy. "Come and look."

Percy hobbled over, using his cane as though he actually needed it. He pulled out his monocle, took off his top hat, and pushed the binoculars up to his eyes.

"Oh, I don't think it works!" Percy called. "Are my eyes really that bad?"

"Other way, dear." Dot took them off him and turned them around. "How did you cope so long without me?"

"I have no idea, Dorothy." Percy pushed his nose up against the glass. "That's him, all right! That's the man! He's getting up. I think he's leaving."

Julia took the binoculars from Percy and watched as the suited man stood. He rested a hand on Jessie's shoulder and said something that made her laugh. Julia's stomach knotted as she watched him pick up a briefcase and head to the door.

"I'm going to talk to him," Julia said, passing the binoculars back to Percy. "He's twice her age!"

Julia welcomed the red mist as she stormed out of Dot's cottage and onto the village green. A lioness roared within her, ready and willing to protect her cub at all costs. The suited man walked out of the café and towards the post office. He stood on the corner next to the red phone box and pulled out his phone. Julia cast an eye into the café, but Jessie was too busy turning off the lights to have noticed her.

"*You there!*" Julia cried, her finger outstretched. "Just what do you think you're doing?"

The man looked up from his phone and squinted at Julia through the darkness. He was nearing his fifties, balding, and too thick around the middle for the size suit he was wearing.

"Excuse me?" he said as he looked her up and down. "You're dressed like a maid."

"I *know* I'm dressed like a maid!" Julia cried as she snatched the bonnet off her head. "Answer my question. What are you doing with my daughter? She's only eighteen!"

"I'm sorry?" The man's brows fell heavier over his eyes. "I don't quite know what you're talking about."

"*Jessie!*" Julia tossed her hand at the café just as the lights switched off. "I just saw you talking to her!"

"Oh, Jessie." The man looked a little less confused as he nodded. "You're her mother?"

"That's what I said!"

"It's nice to meet you. You've raised a good kid

there."

"I know I have!" Julia felt her anger rise within. "Which is why I don't understand what she's doing with you. You're old enough to be her—"

"Whoa, whoa, whoa!" He fanned his hand to calm Julia. "Let me stop you right there. I think there have been some crossed wires. I'm Jessie's estate agent."

Julia took a step back, her heart tightening in her chest.

"What?"

"Estate agent?" The man repeated. "An estate agent is someone who helps people find houses to—"

"I know what an estate agent is!" Julia cried, unsure why she was shouting. "You're Jessie's estate agent?"

The man reached into his jacket pocket and pulled out a small business card that read 'Larry Cornish—King's Estate Agents.' Julia's mouth dried as she stared at the tiny silver writing on the black card.

"I'm—I'm sorry," Julia muttered as she thrust the card back at him. "I—I need to go."

Leaving Larry Cornish outside the post office, Julia hurried back across the green to Dot's cottage before Jessie could leave the café and spot her. Once back in the cottage, she closed the door and leaned against it, staring down Dot's hallway blankly.

"*Well*?" Dot cried, hurrying in, binoculars still in hand. "Who is he?"

"An estate agent." Julia inhaled, but the corset stopped the full breath reaching her lungs. "Jessie doesn't want to live with me anymore. That's why she's been acting so off with me. She's leaving."

Agatha Frost

14

Though she desperately wanted to know why Jessie had decided to leave the cottage, Julia couldn't bring herself to ask. They spent all Monday night putting together a plan for Dot's engagement buffet as though nothing was any different. When Jessie went to bed a little before midnight, Julia intended to talk to Barker about the situation, but she couldn't bring herself to talk to him either. Naively, she thought not talking about it wouldn't make it real, but when she found herself baking cakes for the party at 4am while the cottage slept, it felt far too real indeed.

After a couple of hours of broken sleep, Julia woke early to get Vinnie ready for the day. When Jessie woke to go to the café, Julia hated herself for avoiding her, but she wasn't sure she could look in her eyes without crying.

"What did I do wrong?" Julia asked Dot when they were at the village hall, setting things up for the party later that morning. "I've been wracking my brain trying to figure out what I've done to upset her."

"Oh, Julia, you haven't done anything!" Dot tucked her finger under Julia's chin and lifted her head up. "You've been an amazing mother to that girl, and she knows it. You haven't done a single thing wrong."

"And yet she wants to go."

Julia and Dot set up the last pop-up table for the buffet and stepped back to look at their handiwork. In the space of a couple of hours, the hall had already been somewhat transformed. Dark green velvet lined the walls, and Victorian-era props had been set up all around the room. It looked amazing, but Julia was too distracted to enjoy it.

"She's turning into a young woman," Dot assured her. "Remember being eighteen and feeling like you wanted to take on the world? She's not leaving you behind, she's just spreading her own wings to find out who she is."

"But why would she keep it from me?"

"Why do you think, dear?" Dot cupped Julia's face in her hands. "Forgive me for saying this, but you're not taking this well, are you?"

Julia shook her head. "I don't know how to react."

"Be relieved that it's not something worse." Dot gave Julia's cheeks a squeeze. "*I* feared the worst. I read an awful article about a girl who woke up in a shed in Serbia with her kidney missing! Be thankful it wasn't a kidney!"

Julia allowed herself a smile at her gran's silliness. Even though she could be draining and highly dramatic, Julia appreciated how Dot could always make her laugh, even if she intended to or not.

"I don't want to lose her," Julia said, barely above a whisper. "I've only had her for two years. It's not long enough."

"I don't know how to break this to you, but it's

never long enough, Julia." Dot pulled her over to the stage that had been set up for Percy's magic show, and they sat on the step. "Remember when you left me to go live in London with that awful man? You're my granddaughter, but I raised you as good as my own while your dad ran around the country chasing antiques. I know he didn't cope well with losing your mother, and even though a part of me will never forgive him for abandoning you girls for so long, another part was grateful that he left you with me. I got to be a mother all over again, and I loved every second of it. Don't tell Sue, but you were the easier of the two. I never had to worry about you. You were twenty-three when you left, and I still wasn't ready to let you go. Oh, the nights I would pine for you to come home!"

"You never said anything." Julia suddenly felt guilty, sixteen years too late. "If I'd have known—"

"I never said anything because I didn't want my feelings to impact your decisions," Dot cut her off and slapped her on the knee. "Now, if I'd have known what kind of man Jerrad would turn out to be, I might have put up more of a fight, but it wasn't my place. I had to let you go to live your own life. You needed to go out there to make your mistakes and figure out who you were. And look how you turned out! You're a kind, compassionate, caring, inquisitive, determined woman, and I couldn't be prouder."

"Oh, Gran, I—"

"My *point* is," Dot interrupted again, "who knows who you would have turned out to be if I'd clung to you and not let go. I wanted to, but I didn't. You might be the exact same woman you are now, or you might have turned out completely different. You'd be less resilient, that's for sure. It might have taken you twelve years, but you came home eventually. I always knew you would—I just selfishly hoped you'd come home before I ended up in an urn on your fireplace. If you hadn't that would have been okay too. We get one life, Julia, and it's not as long as you think. The decades go by faster than I like to acknowledge, and it scares the living daylights out of me, not that I let on. I might be eighty-five on the outside, but inside, I can still run for that bus and spring out of bed in the morning, even if my body doesn't quite agree. Let Jessie figure out who she is. If you make her feel guilty about leaving, she might never go, and is that what you really want for her?"

Julia shook her head.

"She'll always be your daughter." Dot tapped

her knee again before standing up. "Whether she's in Peridale or Timbuktu, she'll never really leave you. Now, stop wallowing! I raised you better than that! You're a South woman, act like it!"

With that, Dot marched off to boss around the decorators. Julia sat in the echo of her gran's words, more grateful for her wisdom than she could ever express. Feeling more together, Julia stood and shook away her sorrow. She decided she would talk to Jessie like the adult she was the first chance she got—but until then, she still had a mystery to unravel.

Promising Dot she would be back later with the buffet food, Julia left the village hall and jumped into her car. She pulled out her notepad and pen and flicked to her notes. She circled Camila's name before tossing the notepad onto the passenger seat and setting off. Determined that she would speak to the widow before the day was over, Julia set off in search of her.

She started at the riding school, which felt like the obvious place. Even though it was still within school hours, the yard was busy with the adults and older teens. One of them let Julia in by opening the gate, and she drove in, careful to be vigilant after Florence's story.

"Nice car." Florence slapped the roof after walking over. "Vintage. I like it. Changed your mind about the lessons?"

"Not exactly."

"Don't sweat it." Florence winked. "I asked my mum about you. She remembers every kid she ever taught here before I took over, and Julia South didn't ring a bell with her. Although, she remembered a Sue South."

"Busted." Julia held up her hands. "That would be my sister. I did come here to ride once, but a horse threw me off and put me off for life."

"Wise woman. I can barely feel my buttocks anymore after being thrown off so many times over the years." Florence folded her arms and peered down at Julia. "And that's not to mention the broken bones. So, to what do I owe the pleasure of your visit if you're not here to ride?"

"Camila?" Julia asked. "Is she around?"

Florence sucked the air through her teeth as she shook her head.

"Haven't seen her since you scared her off yesterday."

"Oh."

"That's not unusual," Florence said quickly. "She's not one of those who comes every day. She has more sense than that. She pays for full livery, so we look after her horse, and she drops in when she feels like it."

"How often is that?"

"Couple times a week." Florence shook her head from side to side. "Sometimes less. She's a fair-weather rider, so we only see her when it's dry. She might drop by today, but it's unlikely. I don't think she's ever been two days in a row before. Maybe she'll break the habit of a lifetime, but I doubt it."

Julia considered her next move for a moment. She'd hoped Camila would be waiting for her at the yard, but she hadn't planned what to do if she wasn't.

"Do you know where she lives?" Julia asked.

"Nope." Florence pursed her lips. "And you should know better than to ask me that. You run a café. I could get in trouble for telling you even if I did know. I think she lives in Riverswick, but that's about it. Are you sure I can't tempt you to ride? Samson can be tacked up and ready for you in five minutes. Just say the word."

"Maybe next time."

"Shame." Florence sighed. "I'm bored and quite fancied a laugh. Never mind, eh? Like you said, next time."

"Can you call me if she turns up?" Julia opened her car door and grabbed the pen and pad from the seat. "Here's my mobile and my house number."

"You know them both off by heart?"

"I recently had reason to learn them." Julia tore the paper out of the pad and handed it over. "Please?"

"What's in it for me?" Florence looked at the paper before folding it and pocketing it in her quilted jacket.

"Free coffee and cake next time you're in the village."

"Make it the whole cake, and I'm there."

"Deal." Julia held her hand, and Florence shook it. "Thank you."

Leaving Florence to her horses, Julia drove back up the lane, passing her cottage in the process. She felt bad for leaving Vinnie with Barker, but she knew it was nothing he couldn't handle. Considering where she was heading next, it was for the best that Barker was fully occupied.

Instead of parking in the car park in the middle of Fern Moore, she tucked her car on a quiet country lane ten minutes away. She could see the estate on the horizon, far enough to at least protect her car, but also close enough to run to if she needed to.

Not wanting to risk coming across as a 'Peridale Princess', she dug Barker's black raincoat out of the boot, which had been there since they'd driven three hours north to climb the historic Pendle Hill on one quiet, wet Sunday last summer. She exchanged it for her pink peacoat, zipped it to the chin, and pulled the hood up.

Keeping her head down and her hands in her pockets, Julia walked to the estate as quickly as she dared. She wasn't sure whether she was incredibly stupid or incredibly brave to return less than a week after her previous visit. Either way, she kept her head down as low as she could, letting her feet take her to the stairwell she had escaped up.

She passed the phone box and took the stairs two at a time. The horrible thought that she'd be trapped if the gang were somehow walking down the same stairwell took over her mind, causing her to hold her breath until she reached Addie's floor. She didn't allow herself to glance up until she was at Addie's front door. Pulling her hood down so as not to scare the woman, Julia reached through the bars and knocked. While she waited, she peeked over the edge of the balcony. The playground and courtyard looked empty, with all the shadowy nooks and crannies, she couldn't feel fully at ease.

"Hello?" Addie's familiar voice floated through the chained crack in the door. "Who is it?"

"It's Julia," she replied, unzipping the black coat. "Remember me? I was here last week."

The door closed, and a minute later, the chain rattled, and the door reopened.

"Don't mind me, dear," Addie said as she unlocked the front gate. "Had to pop my teeth in. You'll understand when you get to my age. Do come in."

Addie swung open the gate and stepped to the side, letting Julia in. The *BBC News at One* was playing silently on the television, subtitles running across the bottom of the screen. A cracked open boiled egg sat on the table, with a plate of toast soldiers next to it.

"Have I disturbed your lunch?" Julia asked.

"Oh, it's okay, dear!" Addie ushered Julia further into the flat. "It's better to get these things out of the way. Do you need a pen and paper?"

Addie bent over and opened a small cupboard next to an overstuffed bookcase.

"A pen and paper?" Julia asked.

"For the gas meter reading?" Addie said. "I did

call weeks ago."

Julia's heart panged; the sweet old lady had no idea who she was.

"A pen and paper would be lovely," she said, swallowing the lump in her throat.

Unsure if she was doing the right thing by playing along, Julia let Addie run off to the kitchen to grab her the items. While alone, she crept over to Oliver's bedroom door and knocked, but there was no answer.

"Here you go." Addie returned and handed Julia the pen and paper. "Do you mind if I finish my lunch? You don't need my help."

"No, that's all right."

Julia settled onto her knees on the floral carpet and jotted down Addie's meter readings. She had no idea what she was going to do with them, but she felt compelled to play along since she had come this far. While she was down there, it struck her how easy it would be for someone to lie their way into her flat, even with the gate.

"All done," Julia announced after closing the cupboard door and standing up. "I'll make sure to get these figures sent off to the ... erm ... gas people."

"You do that." Addie wagged her finger above

her head as she squinted at the TV. "I feel like I'm forever topping up the gas! How much could a woman like me really use on her own? The thing must be faulty."

"You live here alone?" Julia asked, fighting the sudden urge to break down and cry. "There are two sets of shoes next to the door. One of them looks like a man's shoes."

"What's that, dear?" Addie glanced over her shoulder.

"Men's shoes?"

"Oh, those will belong to..." Addie scrunched up her face and snapped her fingers repeatedly. "It'll come to me. It's on the tip of my tongue. Old memory isn't what it was. Oh, what was it? Lovely young lad. He's always doing things for me."

"Oliver?"

"*Oliver*!" Addie slapped her hand on the sofa. "That's it! Thank you, dear."

Addie didn't ask how Julia knew her lodger's name. She dunked her toast into her boiled egg and continued reading the words on the screen. Julia softly knocked on Oliver's door again, but there was no answer. She almost told Addie to tell Oliver she'd dropped by, but she knew it would be useless. Instead, she used the pen and paper Addie had given her and scribbled her number on the back of the gas meter numbers along with her name and a message to call her. She slipped it under Oliver's bedroom door.

"I'll be going then."

"Drop by again, dear!" Addie waved over her shoulder. "It was lovely to see you."

Leaving Addie to her eggs and news, Julia slipped out of the flat, closing the door and gate behind her. It hurt to think of anyone losing themselves in such a way, but at least Addie had Oliver there to look after her the best he could.

Pushing Addie's condition to the back of her mind, Julia covered herself up again and set off back to her car. As she hurried across the courtyard, she was sure she heard the grumble of a bunch of teenage boys, but she didn't look up to check. Once she was out of view of the estate, she ran down the lane, not stopping until she was safely back at the car.

Quickly checking her phone let her know Barker wasn't wondering where she was. She felt guilty that he thought she was at the village hall helping Dot all afternoon, but he'd try to stop her if he knew she was running around in search of Camila. She couldn't blame him, but this was something she felt she needed to do, and if it resulted in answers, it would be worth it.

Safely away from the estate, Julia contentedly gathered her thoughts and planned her next move. With Florence not knowing where Camila lived and Oliver not being home, Julia's options were limited. She toyed with the idea of calling Christie to ask, but after his heartfelt confessions at the pub, she doubted he would be in any mood to talk to her. Even with Christie out of the question, there was still a possibility that Oliver would return to Addie's flat and see the note; he might only have run out to grab bread from the shop. On the other hand, he could be out job-hunting and might not get back until after sunset.

Knowing she couldn't sit in the lane waiting for her phone to ring, Julia pushed her keys into the ignition. As she looked down at her handbrake, the notepad on the driver's seat caught her attention. It was open to a page detailing everything Bev had told her.

"It was Bev's home before it was Camila's," Julia thought aloud as she lifted her handbrake and put her car into first gear.

Two out of two times she had visited Little Tots Treasures, Bev had been there. Hoping to make it a lucky three, Julia drove straight there. The car park was almost empty, but the grinning pirate monkey on the side of the building gave her a glimmer of hope that the answers she sought were inside.

After locking her car, Julia walked towards the entrance. Would they find it odd that she was there without a child, or would she be able to lie her way in and say she was waiting for her husband to arrive? Either way, she'd had well over a week to find out Camila's address. She hadn't given the Spanish widow much thought until Christie told her about the PI. Now that it was possible Camila had paid someone to follow Tony, Julia wanted to know what she had uncovered about her husband, and if it was enough to give her a motive to murder.

Despite her worrying, her lie about waiting for her husband didn't raise any eyebrows. She walked straight through to the coffee shop, where two women were sat sipping coffee and scrolling through their phones while their small ones played in the ball pit. Julia was disappointed when she was greeted by the young woman who had left her to go on a break during Julia's first visit.

"Cup of tea, please," Julia ordered as she dug out the change in her purse.

"Milk and sugar?" the girl asked flatly as she punched on the till's screen.

"No, thank you."

After Julia paid, the girl turned to make the tea. When she was finished, she turned back and hit it forcefully on the counter with the laziest fake smile Julia had ever seen.

"Is Bev around?" Julia asked as she scanned the cakes in the display case. "I'm a friend."

"Bev has friends?" The girl snorted. "She quit."

"*Quit*? When?"

"Not much of a friend, are you?" The girl rolled her eyes before blowing a large pink chewing gum bubble. "This morning. Stormed in and made a big song and dance about leaving here to start a new life. Dunno what new life. Maybe she's going back to the farm to join the other pigs?"

The girl found her joke hilarious, but Julia didn't. She stared coldly at the insolent girl, waiting for her to stop laughing. When she finally finished, Julia had developed a newfound respect for Bev. Deep down, she was a nice woman, and yet people were unnecessarily cruel to her.

"Do you know where she lives?" Julia asked, her nostrils flaring.

"Nah." She shook her head while checking her

nails. "I thought you were her friend?"

"Will anyone here know her address?" Julia pushed. "It really is very important."

The girl shrugged, but when she seemed to realise Julia wasn't going to go away until she found out, she rolled her eyes and plodded into the kitchen.

"*Pat*?" she cried, her voice echoing. "Do you know where Bev lives? I know she tried forcing you to be her friend. Did you ever go to her house?"

"Who wants to know?" Pat called back from somewhere within the kitchen.

"Dunno. Some woman. Said she's her friend."

"*Friend*?" Pat called back, a laugh in her voice. "I need to see this."

Pat emerged through the staff door in chef's whites rubbing her hands on a tea towel.

"Are you police?" Pat asked, crossing her thick arms as she stared down her nose at Julia.

"No," Julia replied. "I met Bev recently. Do you know where she lives?"

"Cottage in Riverswick."

"Do you know the house number?"

Pat shrugged.

"Street name?"

Pat shrugged again.

"Anything?"

"Was next to a shop."

"What kind of shop?"

"Bookshop, I think." Pat gave yet another shrug. "I was drunk, and it was dark. I only went once after last year's Christmas party. Pub closed, and she said she had some vodka. Turned out she didn't, so I left."

Julia didn't bother thanking either woman. Leaving her tea behind, she walked to her car, glad Bev had quit working at a place with such horrid people. She had no idea what Bev had planned for her new life, but she hoped it involved surrounding herself with better people.

Once back in her car, Julia checked to see if Oliver had called, but her notification wall was blank. She wasn't too disappointed. Now that she had an idea where Bev lived, she had a hope of finding Camila before the party.

Riverswick, a village like Peridale in size and scale, was another sleepy Cotswold dwelling place with historical cottages built from honey-coloured stone. It was popular with tourists, thanks to the river that ran through the heart of the village, which always had at least one narrowboat floating up and down its calm waters.

Riverswick had a single main shopping road, filled with shops and terraced cottages. A large church and pub capped it off at either end, with many side streets snaking off the main road, some leading to secret shopping hideaways, and others breaking off into the wide-open countryside, with small clusters of cottages dotting the landscape. A tall First World War memorial stood proudly in the middle of the road, with the traffic diverging around it on a roundabout. Whereas Peridale could have its quiet days, Riverswick always seemed to be teeming with life, no doubt thanks to its centralised design. Julia pulled up in a car park hidden behind the pub and set off on her quest to find a cottage next to a bookshop.

What seemed like a simple task at first suddenly became daunting when she realised how many shops had books displayed in their windows. The first, an actual bookshop, had a tea room on one side and a butcher on the other. On the opposite side of the road was a charity shop that had books in the window, but again, had no cottages on either side. Walking further down the road, she kept her eyes peeled, scanning the faces in the street for Bev's. As she walked further down the street, she realised just how many other streets snaked off; there were just as many cottages and shops down them. Julia checked her watch and didn't know how much of the afternoon she could waste in her hunt for Bev's cottage.

She passed the war memorial and crossed the road. The next shop that had books in the window was a gift shop, although the books were notepads and diaries and not books for reading. Still, there was a cottage next door. Julia knocked on the door, hoping Bev would answer and end her search.

The door opened; it wasn't Bev.

"Yes?" a smiley woman in an apron covered in flour asked, a rolling pin in her hand. "Can I help you?"

"Does Bev live here?"

"Bev?" the woman shook her head. "No Bevs here."

Apologising for disturbing her, Julia hurried along. She spotted more books in a coffee shop window. Even though they were stacked as a decorative item, they were books all the same. Julia knocked on the door, but this time received no answer. It wasn't an encouraging sign, but it didn't confirm anything either way. Instead of giving up, she entered the coffee shop, which had the look of a chain coffee shop but the feel of a family-run business.

"Do you know if Bev is home?" Julia pointed her thumb at the wall connecting to the cottage, deciding to lead with confidence. "I knocked, but there was no answer."

"Bev?" the man behind the counter echoed. "I'm sure she was just in here. One second." He craned his neck to look through a beaded curtain. "*Dave*? Was that Bev from next door just in here?"

"Twenty minutes ago," Dave called back. "She was asking for a job."

"There's your answer," the man behind the counter said with a smile. "Can I get you anything else?"

Julia shook her head and returned to the street. She wondered how many places Bev had visited since quitting her job. If she had started at the top, it made sense for the coffee shop to be the final place she asked before retreating to her cottage, unless she continued down the street to the rest of the businesses. Remembering that Bev had experience working in a coffee shop, she concluded that the coffee shop next to her house might have been the only place she'd asked for a job, in which case, she would be at home.

Julia knocked again, louder this time. Not

wanting to draw attention to herself, Julia stood and waited quietly. When nothing stirred within, she walked over to the low front window. Net curtains clouded her vision, but the inside curtains were open. Julia cupped her hands to see if she could see any movement. She couldn't, but she saw a figure sitting in an armchair. She knocked on the window, but the figure didn't move. She knocked again, loud enough to wake Bev up if she was asleep—but how deep a sleep could she have entered in the twenty minutes since she left the coffee shop?

"Bev?" she called as she knocked on the glass. "Bev? Are you okay?"

Bev didn't stir, so Julia didn't waste another second. She burst into the coffee shop.

"I need help!" she cried. "I think something's wrong with Bev."

The man behind the counter hurried around and joined Julia outside. He looked through the window and did his own round of knocking and shouting. When Bev didn't move, the man didn't hesitate in taking his foot to the door. One sharp kick burst the old cottage's lock. Gasps danced around Julia as people gathered to see what was happening.

Pushing past the barista, Julia ran into the small cottage and straight into the sitting room. Bottle of pills in hand, Bev was sunken in her armchair, head lolling to the side and eyes shut.

"What the—" the man started. "She was *just* in the coffee shop! This can't be right!"

"You need to make her empty her stomach!" Julia ordered as she pulled out her phone with shaky fingers. "Do whatever you need to do! I'm going to call an ambulance."

Turning away as the barista opened Bev's mouth, Julia clenched her eyes shut and requested an ambulance. The operator told her one was two minutes away and would be sent right over. Bev retched in the background, letting Julia know there might be a chance of saving her. When the sirens blared outside, the operator hung up, leaving Julia and the barista to step aside. Julia bit one of her fingernails as she watched the paramedics work.

A soft meow came from behind her, making Julia turn around. A tiny white cat with tabby markings jumped onto the dining table. It meowed again and sat on the table edge next to a handwritten note. Julia's heart stopped when she realised what it was. Careful not to touch it, she leaned in and read the scrawled handwriting:

I cannot live on this world anymore without my precious Tony. I thought killing him would fix everything, but it made me realise how much I loved him. I made a mistake. I am sorry. I'm going to join my precious Tony in the afterlife. This is for the best.

The note looked like it had been written in a hurry, but Julia didn't think for a moment it had been written by Bev. She'd heard the phrase 'my precious Tony' before, and it had only left one person's lips.

Turning back to the paramedics as they strapped Bev to a stretcher, she willed her to pull through as her phone rang against her ear.

"Christie? It's Julia."

"*Julia?*" he called down the phone, his voice echoing as though she was on a loudspeaker. "Where are you?"

"I'm at Bev's cottage. It looks like she's taken an overdose."

"*Suicide?*"

"That's how it would appear." Julia glanced at the note again. "Where does Camila live?"

"Julia, you know I can't—"

"*Christie*! Tell me where Camila lives!"

"Stay where you are," he barked. "I'm driving back to the village now, but the traffic is murder! You were right. It wasn't Bev. Forensics have just found something on Tony's computer. An internet search. He tried to delete it, but nothing really deletes on a computer."

"An internet search?"

"The day after he accepted the offer to judge the bake-off, he was looking up some strange things."

"How strange?"

"He wanted to know how many peanuts would harm but not kill someone with an allergy if they were immediately administered with an EpiPen," Christie called over the sound of a honking horn. "Listen, I think it was a stitch-up gone wrong. I think Tony wanted to create a situation where he could sue the organisers for a lot of money. He was looking at articles from similar cases. The man was in a lot of debt."

"Camila was supposed to have the EpiPen in her bag," Julia said. "Christie, are you going to tell me where she lives?"

"Julia, you know I—"

Julia hung up and tossed her phone into her

bag. She hurried over to Bev as the paramedics picked up the stretcher to carry her out to the ambulance.

"Is she alive?" Julia asked.

"Just," one of the paramedics said. "Do you know how many pills she might have taken?"

"No." Julia shook her head. "And she didn't take them. Not willingly, at least. This is an attempted murder. If she comes around at any moment, ask her who it was."

Looking confused, the paramedics nodded as they carted Bev out. Leaving the barista shell-shocked in Bev's sitting room, Julia jogged back to her car at the top of the street. If Christie wasn't going to tell her where Camila lived, she would find out for herself, and there was only one person left to ask.

Agatha Frost

15

For the second time in a day, Julia found herself at the Fern Moore estate, but this time, she drove right up to the car park in front of the courtyard. She didn't have time to be extra safe. If she hadn't taken such precautions last time, she might have ended up at Bev's cottage before Camila had a chance to force pills down her throat. Jumping out her car in her pink peacoat, she dared anyone to try confronting her, considering the mood she was in.

Luckily for Julia, no gangs lurked, leaving her

to make her way easily up to Addie's flat. Before she reached the front door, her phone rang in her pocket. It was an unknown number, which gave her a glimmer of hope.

"Julia?" a familiar voice called through the phone. "I've just got back and seen your note. Is everything okay?"

"I'm outside your front door. Come out, and I'll explain everything."

Julia hung up, relieved that she finally had a key to finding Camila's whereabouts. She waited impatiently while Oliver unlocked the inside door and then the gate. His face was red, and his hair drenched with sweat. He wore a tight sports t-shirt, which hugged his slender frame, and matching tight leggings poking out under a pair of baggier shorts. A pair of white earbud headphones were pulled through the top of his shirt, resting against his chest.

"Oh." Oliver laughed. "I've just been for a run. Helps keep me sane. What's going on? I tried to ask Addie, but she doesn't even remember you coming around. She has good days and bad days."

"That's why I left the note," Julia said, her voice low. "I didn't want to risk you not getting back to me. I've been running around all morning trying to find out where Camila lives, and now it's more important than ever."

"Camila?" Oliver replied with a confused look. "She lives in Riverswick."

"I've just come from Riverswick." Julia exhaled and grabbed at her hair. "I've just been at Bev's cottage on the main road. She—she's on her way to hospital."

"Bev?" Oliver frowned. "What's happened? Is she all right?"

"I don't know." Julia's heart fluttered in her chest. "I hope so. I think Camila just tried to murder Bev and frame her for Tony's murder all at once. What's her address?"

"I—I don't know."

"You don't know?"

"Not the street name or house number, but I know which house it is. I could point it out to you."

"I can't ask you to do that." Julia grabbed both of Oliver's arms and looked him dead in the eye. "It could be dangerous."

"If it's dangerous, why are you running towards it?"

"Because I need to know the truth." Julia sighed heavily and dropped her head. "I've come this far, and I need answers."

"And you don't think I want answers, too?" Oliver pulled himself away from Julia. "I worked for those people for a year, and I watched one of them die. I'm coming with you. Give me ten seconds. I need to explain to Addie that I'm going out again."

Feeling uneasy about involving a kid in her silly game of cat and mouse, Julia stepped back and leaned against the balcony. She rubbed her forehead before checking her phone. To her surprise, no one had tried to call or text her, which meant Christie was too busy to let Barker know what she was doing. She thought about texting Barker a lie so he didn't worry, but she immediately dismissed the idea. As it stood, she hadn't lied to him yet. She'd told him she was leaving the cottage to help Dot at the village hall, and that's what she had done before the afternoon escaped her.

Oliver hurried out of the flat, now with a burgundy hoodie over his running gear. He locked the door and gate behind him before they hurried to Julia's car. As she reversed away, she spotted a gang of teenage boys. She couldn't be sure that they were the group who had mugged her, but it looked a lot like them, not that it mattered at that moment; she had bigger fish to fry than her missing possessions.

She got all the way to the bridge over the river that signalled they were entering Riverswick before Oliver began his directions. Instead of heading to the part of town where Julia had just been, they headed further west, to the large detached houses with huge plots of their own land.

"It's just up here." Oliver pointed. "It's the last one on the right."

Julia pulled up outside the large detached cottage, which looked more modern than most in the small Cotswold villages. It had perfectly neat green hedges and a white gravel driveway leading up to a grand red door centred between two large windows. Its square structure, lack of traditional golden Cotswold stone, and perfectly straight roof hinted that it hadn't been there a century ago.

"You have to wait here," Julia ordered as she opened her door.

"But—"

"No buts," Julia insisted. "I'm not letting you walk into this. You're a kid, Oliver. You have your whole life ahead of you. If I'm not out in ten minutes, call the police, okay?"

"Be careful, yeah?" he said as he gave her a

quick smile.

"I always am." Julia climbed out and slammed the door. "Ten minutes."

Leaving Oliver on watch, Julia strode up to the front door. She hadn't had much time to compile her evidence, but the suicide note and the revelation that Tony had wanted to be fed peanuts at the bake-off was all she needed. Camila might have been a good actress, but there was no way she wouldn't crack when Julia dropped those bombshells.

After ringing the doorbell, Julia turned back to Oliver. She gave him a wave, and he returned it. If time hadn't been against them, Julia would have driven Oliver back home now that she knew where Camila lived.

Heels clicked along wood flooring, signalling that Julia's time had come. She straightened up and tucked her curls behind her ears. The door swung open, and, as she'd hoped, Camila finally stood before her.

"Oh, hello," Camila said as she put an earring in. "Julie, isn't it?"

"Julia," she corrected her for the first time. "Can I come in? You've been a difficult woman to track down."

Without waiting for Camila to answer, Julia strode deep enough down the hallway to put distance between them. While Camila closed the door, Julia looked around. The cottage was beautiful, but it missed a homely touch. The walls were completely bare, and the little furniture there was scattered around; it felt like a show home.

"Is now a bad time?" Julia asked, walking into the sitting room, which was just as bare as the hallway.

"Well, yes, actually." Camila followed Julia in as she put a matching earring in the other side. "It's my birthday. I wasn't going to celebrate, but my friends made me promise I would at least go and eat with them. It's the last thing I want to do, but I know they only want to help since my precious Tony isn't here to celebrate with me."

"Ah, yes." Julia nodded, glancing into the dining room, which was completely empty aside from a bare bookcase. "Your precious Tony. So precious that you had him followed by a private investigator."

"How—I—"

"Nigel Bell?" Julia interrupted. "Don't try to deny it. I know."

Camila glared at Julia from the doorway of the

sitting room. She had a look in her eye that made Julia feel like a scurrying spider invading her space. A quick glance out the window at her aqua blue car centred her.

"I confess!" Camila held her hands up. "Yes, I had Tony followed. I wanted to be sure."

"That he was cheating on you?"

"That he *wasn't* cheating on me." Camila snapped. "What wife wants their husband to cheat on them?"

"One looking for a motive for murder."

Julia let the words linger in the air. Camila's eyes widened, and her lips parted, but she seemed at a loss for words. It wasn't the reaction Julia had expected, but it was a reaction, nonetheless.

"I know about Tony's nutty idea, if you'll pardon the pun, to contaminate a cake at the bake-off so he could sue them. Looking around, it's obvious you were having money troubles."

"This is true." Camila nodded, her arms folding across her chest as she looked around the bare room. "One by one, Tony sold our precious things to pay the bills. He said it would be better to live in an empty house as beautiful as this than move somewhere beneath us with all this stuff, but now that's he's gone, I know neither is true. I would live anywhere with my precious Tony if it meant he could come back to me."

"So, you knew about his plan to ruin the bake-off?"

Camila's eyes narrowed on Julia, but she eventually nodded.

"I told him he was crazy!" she cried, tossing her arms out. "It wasn't worth it. I talked him out of it. He promised he wouldn't do it."

"And yet, he did." Julia walked a couple steps across the empty sitting room, so there was nothing between them but the single black leather sofa in the middle of the room. "And you were supposed to rush in with his EpiPen to save the day. It didn't matter that he'd had to go through that because it meant he could sue, and he'd probably get a lot of money for it. Allergies like that are very serious."

"I think you should leave!" Camila cried, pointing to the hallway. "How *dare* you!"

"Give it up, Camila." Julia pulled the pictures of the PI out of her bag. "It all makes sense now. You had Tony followed, found out about his cheating, and used his crazy scheme against him. You were supposed to have the EpiPen, but you hid it under the coats so no one would find it in time to save him. Bev turning up was the icing on the cake. It meant you could frame her, but it didn't work, did it? That's why you went to her cottage this afternoon and forced pills down her throat. You wrote that suicide note thinking it would clear your name, but you only made things worse for yourself! My precious Tony? You might as well have signed your name at the bottom!"

"What are you talking about?" Camila cried as she snatched up the pictures. "Nigel Bell didn't find *anything*! Nigel followed him for six months and didn't find a single thing! I used all my savings to make sure he loved me like he said he did. Tony was faithful to me! And Bev? I know nothing of this suicide note! I don't even know where Bev lives! Where did you get these images? I have never seen these."

"Tony took them because he knew he was being followed. They were in Tony's emails."

"What emails?" Camila cried, shaking the sheets. "Are you working for the police?"

"No, I—"

"Then how do you have access to Tony's emails?" Camila stepped forward, her eyes turning manic. "What are you doing here, café lady?"

"Tony was using his assistant's laptop."

"What laptop?"

"When Tony's broke. He took Oliver's. You got it back for him."

"None of this *happened*!" Camila screwed up the papers and tossed them at Julia. "You are a *fantasist*! Get out of my house!"

"I—I don't understand." Julia shook her head. "It all points to you."

"*I* don't understand!" Camila pulled her phone from her pocket. "I'm calling the police. You're *crazy*! How *dare* you come here and say these things to me?"

Camila hesitated before dialling the number, her eyes glued on Julia as though waiting for her to pounce. Julia looked out of her window at her car.

"No," she whispered to herself. "It can't be."

"What can't be?"

"I need to make a call." Julia stepped out of the view of the window and retrieved her own phone. "Camila, you can call the police all you want, but can you wait thirty seconds? I'm sorry for everything I said. All I ask is for thirty more seconds of your time."

"Thirty seconds." Camila relaxed her arm and put the phone by her side. "I am counting."

Julia scrolled through her recent contacts and

clicked the number of one of her oldest friends. She pressed the phone against her ear, and, as she expected, the person on the other end picked up almost immediately.

"*Johnny*? It's Julia."

"Oh, hi. I just got an invitation to your—"

"I don't have long, Johnny, just be quiet and listen." Julia inhaled. "What do you know about your cousin, Oliver?"

"I told you, I don't really—"

"I know, you don't know him, but you *must* know *something*." Julia clenched her eyes shut. "Think Johnny. This is important."

"Julia, I don't know what to say. My mum wasn't close to my Auntie Judith. I didn't even know she—"

"Auntie *Judith*?" Julia's eyes sprung open. "As in, Judy?"

"She hates being called that."

"Who's Oliver's dad?"

"No idea. If you'd let me finish, I didn't even know my mum had a sister until about fifteen years ago. They hated each other. Julia, what's going on?"

"Johnny, I'll explain later. Thank you."

She hung up and clutched her phone against

her chin as she stared into space. After ten seconds of putting the correct pieces together, Julia looked up at Camila, who seemed more confused than ever.

"Please, forgive me." Julia grabbed her hands. "I said some awful things. I was wrong."

"What is happening?"

"What did you know about Tony's first wife?"

"Judy?" Camila frowned. "He said she was a horrid woman. She was pregnant, but she lost the baby because—"

"Did Tony say he was there when Judy lost the baby?"

Camila thought for a moment before shaking her head. "I don't think so. He said he came home one day to a note telling him what had happened. He never saw her again."

"Not even during the divorce?" Julia pushed. "What about in court?"

"She didn't show up, and Tony was the one who filed, so the judge granted the divorce without her being there. Julia, what does any of this have to do with Tony's death?"

"I don't think Judy lost that baby." Julia's heart throbbed in her throat at saying the crazy theory out loud. "I think she wanted to get Tony out of her life, so she told him something unforgivable and then vanished."

"Where is this baby?" Camila cried, tears filling her eyes. "You're saying Tony lives on in a child?"

"Oh, Camila, don't get too excited." Julia passed her a tissue from her handbag. "I think you've already spent a year with the child, and it was long enough for him to realise he hated Tony enough to kill him."

"*Who*?" Camila shrieked. "What child? *Tell me!*"

"Oliver." The name almost jammed in Julia's throat. "Tony's assistant."

"It can't be!"

"Call the police," Julia called as she ran into the hall. "I need to talk to him."

Julia opened the door and steadied herself the best she could. She walked to her car, staring at Oliver through the windows. He had both hands in his hoodie pocket, and he was staring off into space as though he didn't have a care in the world. Julia knocked on the window, making him jump.

She opened the car door and climbed in, sure he could hear her heart pounding.

"What happened?" Oliver asked. "Did she confess?"

"No," Julia shook her head. "But don't worry. I

know she's lying. I tied her up and called the police myself. They shouldn't be far off."

"Are you okay?" Oliver asked. "You look like you're—"

"Who's your father, Oliver?" Julia interrupted, turning to face the teenage boy. "I need to know."

Oliver stared back, his brows tilted as though he had just heard some terrible news. It was that expression that had made Julia trust him without question. He had reminded her so much of Jessie, but Jessie's expression had never dropped as readily as Oliver's did. He pulled his hands out of his pockets, and, with them, a large knife, no doubt snatched from Addie's kitchen.

"Drive," he said coldly, resting the knife against her neck.

"Where to?" Julia asked as she turned the key in the ignition.

"I'll direct you."

Agatha Frost

16

Oliver eventually lowered the knife from Julia's throat, but he kept it pointed at her under the dashboard and out of view of other drivers. When they first left Camila's home in Riverswick, they passed two police cars, and even though Julia begged them with her eyes to understand what was going on, none of the officers made eye contact. She did the same thing to every car that passed until it grew too dark to see any faces behind the dazzling headlights.

Julia's phone rang off the hook for the first ten minutes until Oliver snapped at her to switch it off. She did as Barker showed her with the side button and put it on silent, but before she could even think about sending any messages, Oliver seized it and tossed it into the back.

For what felt like hours, Oliver directed Julia with a calm and firm voice. With each turn down never-ending, winding roads, she felt like Oliver had no idea where he was going until she realised they were heading deeper and deeper into the countryside and away from civilisation. It crossed Julia's mind that Oliver might be driving her to her death, but if he had wanted to kill her, he could have done it any number of ways since leaving Riverswick. He was taking her somewhere, and even though neither of them had said anything other than asking for and giving directions, the silence in the air said enough; the police were looking for them, and they both knew it.

With Oliver's knife still pointed at her, Julia stole a glance at the clock on the dashboard. It read 7:13pm, but she'd meant to put it back since daylight savings in October, so it was really 6:13pm. She felt silly for thinking about it, but

Dot's party would be starting in less than twenty minutes. Despite her complaints yesterday, she would have given anything to be caged up in her maid's costume instead of driving into oblivion.

"Pull up by that wall," Oliver ordered, pointing the knife at a stone wall at the end of the lane. "We'll walk the rest of the way."

Was he putting distance between them and the car? Did he think Julia would have a chance of escaping wherever they were going? Was he tricking whoever eventually found the car so they wouldn't find her body easily? Knowing all were possible, she parked where instructed and twisted the keys in the ignition.

"Get out," he ordered. "Leave the keys in here. Don't try to run. I will be able to catch you."

Julia didn't doubt it. She tossed her keys into the footwell and climbed out. To her surprise, Oliver didn't tell her to leave her handbag, so she left is slung over her shoulder. She expected him to notice it immediately when they met around the front of the car, but he didn't seem able to look at her.

"Walk," he ordered, jerking the knife towards a narrow passage in the wall. "I'll direct you."

With only the light of the moon to guide her,

Julia walked forward, feeling for a hardly used path under her feet. She didn't dare look around, but there was nothing ahead of her for miles. No lights, no sound, no one to hear her screams but the motionless trees.

They walked for so long that Julia's feet began to hurt. She didn't dare ask where they were going in case her voice startled Oliver; she was very aware of the blade behind her. Just when Julia was beginning to accept that Oliver was walking her into the middle of nowhere to hide her body, the outline of a structure came into view. It was nothing more than a manmade shadow in the sea of natural silhouettes at first, but the closer they got, she realised it was a farmhouse, and they were walking towards it.

Any hope of Julia being rescued by the inhabitants was quickly dashed because there weren't any. While the structure was large and still mostly intact, it was obvious no one had lived there for a long time. Most of the windows had been smashed, and the front door was missing. Nature had long since started reclaiming the space.

"Inside," he ordered. "Go straight ahead into the kitchen."

Julia did as she was told. To her surprise,

Oliver finally lowered the knife and vanished into another room, giving Julia enough time to reach into her bag and tuck the flashlight up her sleeve. It was nothing compared to the knife, but it was something. She heard some rummaging before Oliver returned less than thirty seconds later carrying two giant duffel bags. He dumped them on the kitchen table next to Julia, sending up a cloud of dust into the dark.

Tucking his knife into his hoodie pocket, Oliver picked up the edge of a blanket covering something in the corner. A flurry of thick dust filled the air, clearing to reveal an old rusty motorbike.

"You're prepared," Julia said, feeling braver without the knife pointing at her. "You planned all this out."

"I didn't plan for *you* to find out like you did." Oliver cast an eye at Julia, but his attention was occupied by the bike. "I'd hoped to be long gone before anyone got close to pointing the finger at me, but I knew I couldn't leave until someone was charged. I didn't intend for you to find Bev. She was supposed to be found in a couple weeks' time when the neighbours started noticing the smell. By then, interest would have died down, and I would have been long gone. The suicide note would have closed the case."

"And just in case they didn't believe that, you wrote the letter as though you were Camila pretending to be Bev," Julia added. "*My precious Tony.*"

"Of course, *you* spotted that." Oliver let out a chuckle. "You really are quite brilliant, Julia. Although, not that brilliant. You didn't realise you were being manipulated. You're too trusting. I realised that from the moment you tried to give me that coffee in the tent. I was trying my best to be the fragile assistant who blended into the walls, but you noticed me right away and wanted to give me my moment. I appreciated that. Who knows, in another life I could have been your Jessie."

"Who knows," Julia said.

Oliver stopped fiddling with the bike. He climbed on and started it. It took a couple of attempts, but the old engine roared. Satisfied with his work, he turned it off and climbed down.

"She told me all about everything you've done for her when she drove me home," Oliver called over his shoulder. "You really are quite special."

"It didn't have to be this way," Julia said, her heart breaking. "You didn't have to kill him."

"Oh, I did." Oliver walked to the bags on the

table and rifled through them. "I have enough food and money to survive in the wild until I figure out something more long-term." He zipped the bags up and looked Julia right in the eye. "You're dying to know why, aren't you? I can tell. Take a seat, and I'll explain. It won't make much difference in the long run."

"Are you going to kill me?"

"No." Oliver shook his head. "But I can't let you live. I have a plan for you. You'll suffer, and I'm sorry for that, but it's the only way. If I let you go, you'll lead them here, and it'll be a starting point for them. It's more than they have right now. Doesn't it feel great to be so off the grid that no one has a clue we're here?" Oliver pulled out two chairs from the old table and motioned for Julia to sit. "I'll explain everything. Think of it as my way of apologising. I really do like you, Julia."

Not wanting to disobey, Julia sat down, clinging the flashlight tight against her sleeve with the ends of her fingers; all she needed was one moment.

"Where to start?" Oliver drummed his fingers on the table. "How about my mother? Judy Bridges, or Judith Smith, as she eventually went by. I grew up with the world's worst mother, and I had no idea who my father was. All of that was true. She would leave me for weeks, months, years on end, and she'd run off to God knows where doing God knows what. Drugs? Men? Hiding? I didn't know, I just know she wasn't there, and the times she was, she was so drunk I wished she wasn't."

Oliver inhaled and ran his fingers down his face, his eyes wide.

"She showed up on my sixteenth birthday. Drunk, of course. I hadn't seen her for a year. I'd been staying with one of my school teachers. Can you imagine that? I was so pathetic, a teacher took me in and looked after me because my mother didn't want to. We were having a birthday dinner, and she turned up. She had a habit of knowing where I was, and she could always pick the perfect moment to come back and ruin things. Whenever I started to feel settled or somewhere close to happy, she'd crash in and ruin everything. That's when she told me about my father."

"Tony Bridges."

"She yelled 'You have a famous daddy!', a cigarette in one hand and a bottle of vodka in the other. I didn't believe her until she grabbed my laptop and typed in their names. Tony and Judy, the darlings of lunchtime news, until they were fired. For the first time in sixteen years, I had some hope. I knew I'd never have a mother, but I had a father out there."

"So, you came and found him?"

"Not right away." Oliver shook his head. "I was scared. I started listening to his radio show every afternoon. I thought he was so nice. I fantasised about the life we would have together. It was going to be perfect. I packed all my things in my bag, and I went to Riverswick to find him. It wasn't difficult. He lived there, he recorded the show there. I watched him for months while I slept rough. The longer I left it, the harder it became to approach him. He didn't know I existed. How could I drop into his life like that? I needed to make him like me first."

"But that never happened."

"It should have happened, but it didn't." Oliver sighed and rubbed his temples. "I was following him around a supermarket. I did that quite often. Blending in was easy. People would go up to him for pictures and autographs all the time. I was just another kid in the shop—until I overheard him on the phone. He was telling someone that Camila had quit being his assistant. I knew that she was his wife, and I knew it was my chance. I went to the library every day and used the free computers to stalk the radio website for the job advert. It took weeks, but, finally, it popped up. I had everything ready to apply, so I know I was the first. I just needed to get an interview. I knew he'd hire me. How could he not? I was his son!"

Oliver leaned back in the chair, his eyes glazing over as he circled his finger around in the dust.

"Tony was awful to me from that first interview," he continued. "I thought once he warmed to me, he'd become the Tony I knew from the radio. That guy was my dad, the other one was someone else. The harder I tried, the more he pushed me away, and the harder it became to tell him the truth. I burrowed deeper and deeper into his life, thinking I could find something I could use to make us connect. I hacked his emails, tracked his online searches, I even bugged his phone. I'd work twelve, sometimes fourteen hours for him, and then I'd go home and go over everything, hoping for a shred of anything I could use. Some common ground to start a real conversation."

"And did that happen?"

"Never." Oliver's eyes darkened. "I learned what I'd been trying to ignore. He was a cruel, nasty loser. I stopped wanting him to like me. I *wanted* him to hate me. He was just as bad as my mother, but at least she had the decency to ruin my life only periodically. Tony was doing it every day, all day. When I saw that he was searching online to see how far he could push his allergy, I knew I had my chance. All I'd have to do was hide the EpiPen. It would have been so easy, but the night before the bake-off, Camila convinced Tony not to go through with it. I found the peanut oil in the bin the next day at the radio station. I knew what I had to do. When Tony left to change his shirt after that woman threw coffee on him, I poured the whole thing onto Bev's pre-cut slice, and then I brought him a fresh shirt. It was too easy. Everyone was flapping around panicking about Tony and the coffee. I worried about the EpiPen because Tony always carried it in his pocket, but I don't think Camila trusted him that morning, so she put it in her bag. All I had to do was bend over, push it up my sleeve, and hide it somewhere. It played out exactly as I expected. Well, I didn't expect to be caught, but I planned for it all the same. I didn't expect to have someone like *you* leading the police in all the right directions. When you turned up at Addie's flat, I knew you had to be dealt with."

"That's why you showed me the EpiPen," Julia

cut in. "To disarm me. You were bluffing."

"And you fell for it."

"You're a good liar."

"You learn to be with parents like mine." Oliver offered an apologetic shrug. "When you invited me to the café to help you piece together Tony's life, it felt like a golden opportunity I couldn't pass up. I had to throw you off. I gave you everything you wanted. Evidence for Bev and Camila—and I even dropped in that horsewoman. I knew it was a possibility that you'd rule all of them out and come after me, but it would at least keep you busy until I could come up with something else."

"And that something else was to kill Bev, make it look like suicide, throw in Camila for extra insurance, and ride off into the sunset with your motorbike and supplies?"

"Exactly." Oliver stood and picked up the bags. "I thought you'd put those pieces together when you turned up at Addie's flat, and I was out of breath. I ran all the way from Bev's cottage." Oliver looked pleased with himself. "Tony wasn't paying me much but living rent-free for a year means I've got a couple of thousand in cash to get me far enough away from here."

"Rent-free?"

"You only need to *tell* Addie you've paid her the rent." Oliver sighed. "Poor woman. I'm going to miss her."

"That's cruel."

"*Cruel*?" Oliver's expression twisted. "I've been looking after her for the past year when no one else would! You know she has two sons, not that she remembers them most of the time. I never saw them once in that year! I was there every single day."

"And robbing her blind?"

"I did what I had to do." Oliver carried the bags over to the motorbike. "If it's any consolation, I doubt she'll even remember me this time next week."

Any shred of empathy and compassion Julia still felt for Oliver dissipated with that final comment. She clung to the flashlight tighter, knowing her moments to use it were running away from her.

"What now?" Julia asked, standing up as Oliver strapped the bags to the bike.

"I drive off and never look back."

"I was talking about me."

"Oh, right." Oliver chuckled. "Well, you'll be going down into the basement. I don't know what you'll find down there, but it should be pretty quiet. I'd say three weeks without food and water is long enough, don't you?"

"Long enough for what?"

Oliver pushed the dining table out of the way and ripped up a dust-covered rug. Julia coughed and wafted. Even if she wanted to use the torch, the cloud between them would dim the effects. She waited for the dust to settle, and when it did, Oliver yanked on a wooden door to reveal a ladder down to the basement.

"Well, she's not making any noise." Oliver skewed his ear into the dark. "I'd say Mother is almost certainly dead."

"Your *mother*?"

"Turned up three weeks ago." Oliver huffed, planting his hands on his hips. "Drunk, of course. Begging for a second chance. She somehow tracked me down to Addie's flat. It was almost too easy to lure her out here. I wasn't going to let her ruin my one shot to kill Tony. I guess this means I'm going to get away with killing *both* of my parents, huh? What are the odds? Well, I suppose this is it. Down you go." He retrieved the knife from his hoodie pocket. "If you don't put up a fight, I won't use this. Maybe someone will stumble upon you. I stumbled upon this place after all. I'm sure someone will be along in a week or two—if you can still scream out for help by then."

Julia stared at the knife as her fingers touched the cold metal of the torch. Was it bright enough to dazzle him and somehow flee? It had almost knocked her off her stool when Barker had demonstrated it, but she'd been half-asleep. Would it have the same effect on a teenage boy with a crazed, and yet lucid, look in his eyes?

"C'mon, Julia." Oliver pointed the knife into the hole. "Don't make me kill you. I didn't mind the others because they weren't important, but it would really upset me if I had to…"

Oliver's voice trailed off and his head whipped to the open front door. It took Julia's older ears a second longer, but she heard it too. The distant but unmistakable blare of police sirens. It was the moment Julia had been waiting for. She dropped the torch into her hand and sent its full beam through the dusty darkness and into Oliver's eyes. The shock made him cry out and shield his face. The knife clattered from his hand and dropped, echoing to let them know it had fallen into the basement and out of reach.

Inspired by the knife, Julia grabbed the loose

fabric of Oliver's hoodie and pulled him towards her. As expected, the teen barely weighed a thing and fell into the hole with little effort. Before he had a chance to gain his bearings and find the knife in the dark, Julia slammed the door shut, and with a strength she hadn't known she possessed, she flipped the heavy dining table and dropped its flat side onto the door. Standing on the table as it rattled underneath her, Julia scrambled in her handbag. She set off the panic alarm, drowning out Oliver's screams. Not wanting to risk not being heard, Julia pressed the whistle against her dry lips and blew like her life depended on it.

She didn't stop whistling when she saw torches dancing through the dark in the distance, nor did she stop when those torches turned to footsteps in the corridor right in front of her eyes. It took Barker pulling the whistle from her hands to break her from her trance.

"Told you they'd come in handy," Barker called over the sound of the blaring panic alarm as he squeezed Julia tight. "Where is he?"

"In the basement with his mother."

"*Mother*?" Christie cried, panting as a small army of uniformed officers followed behind.

"Judy Bridges, or Judith Smith, depending on

who you ask." Julia melted into Barker's chest. "How did you know I was here?"

"Your phone." Barker clutched her head in his hands. "I put the tracker on when you were in the shower that first day you set it up. I promise I didn't look at it until Christie called to tell me what you told him."

"Thank you," Julia whispered. "Bev?"

"She's alive," Christie said as two officers picked up the table Julia had thrown on her own. "Only just, though. She managed to give us Oliver's name, but by then, Camila had already called and told us about your crazy visit. Couldn't help getting into a car with a boy you knew was a killer, could you, Julia?"

"What can I say?" Julia let go of Barker and smiled at Christie with the last of her energy. "I needed to know for sure. Be careful with him, he has a knife down there."

"I brought this." Barker reached into his back pocket and tossed the canister of pepper spray to Christie. "Have fun."

"Oh, with the rings this kid has had me running around in?" Christie shook up the canister as two officers braced themselves to open the trap door. "With pleasure."

Leaving the officers to do their work, Barker walked Julia out of the house and back along the path, which felt so much shorter with a little light in her eyes and without a knife behind her.

"What were you thinking?" Barker whispered when they were almost back at the cars. "I could have lost you ... again."

"I underestimated him," Julia replied. "Take me home, Barker. I'll explain everything when I'm in front of our fire, and I have a cup of peppermint and liquorice tea in my hands.

17

Dot cancelled the party the moment she heard Julia had driven off in her car with a murderer. Not one to waste good costumes though, she rearranged it for Saturday, giving all the other villagers a chance to gather their own outfits. By half past seven on Saturday night, the village hall was bursting with so many perfect costumes, it would be difficult to argue that Dot hadn't transported the whole village back to the 19th century.

"*To Julia!*" Dot gave the first toast of the night. "For saving the day once again, and for not dying, but coming very close more times than she'd like to admit."

All glasses in the hall raised to her, and she accepted it humbly. Since Oliver's arrest for the murders of Tony and Judy, the attempted murders of Bev and Julia, and for trying to frame Camila along the way, people had been taking bets on how many years the judge was going to give him. Wild figures had been thrown around, and even though people like Barker and Christie assured everyone that it wouldn't be possible for the judge to give Oliver a 'whole life sentence' because he was under twenty-one, it didn't stop people speculating that he'd never see the light of day again. In reality, Julia knew Oliver could be walking the streets again in as few as fifteen years, or thirty if the judge was feeling extra tough. With Oliver's background and parents, she doubted the judge would fully throw the book at him, but she didn't expect to be bumping into him in the street any time soon.

The one downside to Oliver's arrest was that there was no one to take care of Addie, although Julia had informed social services about her situation, and they'd promised they would do all they could to assist her.

One of the few positives to come out of the whole ordeal was Bev's turnaround. Staring death in the face had given her the new lease of life she had been looking for since the end of her marriage to Tony. Julia had been over the moon when Bev had told her she had booked a one-way ticket to France to explore the world before it was too late.

"Where's Barker?" Dot called into Julia's ear over the noise of the gramophone. "Percy's magic show starts soon."

"He had to take a phone call," Julia called back, although she didn't have the breath to shout given the tightness of the corset under her maid's outfit. "I think it was his publishers."

"Phone … call?" Dot fanned herself. "I'm not sure I understand, dear. You see, in the simple times that I'm from, they aren't quite household items yet."

"You're really getting into your character, aren't you?"

"Character?" Dot fiddled her brooch. "I don't know what you mean."

Dot floated off to spread the word that Percy would soon begin his magic show. Leaving the noise of the hall behind, Julia snuck out. Barker was sitting on a bench in front of the church.

"Sir, may I get you anything?" Julia asked, curtseying as she fluttered her lashes. "Anything at all?"

Barker laughed deeply as he patted the empty space next to him. In keeping with Julia's service role, Barker had adopted the outfit of a chimney sweep, although Dot had pointed out more than once that he was far too big to fit up any chimney.

"The publishers have scrapped the book."

"Oh, Barker!" Julia clasped his hand. "I'm *so* sorry!"

"No, it's a good thing." Barker squeezed her hand and smiled. "They only scrapped it because I presented them with a new idea. With Oliver's killing spree making national headlines thanks to his parents' faded celebrity status, the publishers practically bit my hand off when I told them the pitch for the book. *The Body at the Bake-Off.* Catchy, right?"

"But you worked so hard on the other book."

"It's okay," he assured her. "I'm ready to let it go. It wasn't meant to be. I have a good feeling about this new idea. Besides, they've offered me a five-figure bonus if I have the first draft on their desk in two weeks."

"*Two weeks*?" Julia cried. "That's impossible! How are you going to do that?"

"With a lot of coffee and not a lot of sleep, so I'm afraid you're going to have to miss me for a little while longer. But after that, I'm all yours." Barker leaned in and kissed her. "We can even go on a nice, long honeymoon and spend that bonus in style. But let's not think about that right now! Let's get back in there and party like it's 1879!" He stood and pulled Julia up with him. "I'll meet you inside. I think you're needed out here."

Barker nodded across the churchyard to the shadowy figure of another maid sitting on the wall. When she was alone, Julia approached Jessie, who had dressed as a maid in solidarity.

"Don't let the mistress catch you slacking out here," Julia said as she sat on the lumpy wall next to Jessie. "I wouldn't be surprised if Dot comes out to cane us for not passing drinks around. She's been consumed by her Victorian ancestors."

Jessie laughed, but Julia could tell her heart wasn't in it. It had been five days since Julia had confronted the estate agent dressed in the same costume, and for every one of those five days, she'd wanted to talk to Jessie about it. Now that they were alone in the chilly night, it felt like the right time.

"Jessie, I—"

"Here." Jessie reached into her frilly apron and put something in Julia's hand. "I found them."

Julia opened her hand and stared, mouth agape, at three items she'd given up all hope of ever seeing again.

"*My jewellery*!" Julia cried, clenching the pieces tightly in her fist. "How—why—I don't understand."

"You hang around Fern Moore long enough, twist the right arms, and people start talking." Jessie shrugged as though it was nothing. "They didn't even know what to do once they had them. When I found Mark, it only took me a couple days to track them down."

"You confronted them?"

Jessie nodded. "I hope you don't mind, but I gave Mark a black eye. I made sure he knew why he was getting it, too. He apologised while he cried like a baby. I thought it would be satisfying, but he was just pathetic. They don't scare me. They're nothing but kids pretending to be gangsters. People like Oliver scare me. I ended up liking him."

"I liked him, too."

"I thought we were the *same*."

"You're nothing alike." Julia wrapped her arm around Jessie's shoulders. "Nothing alike."

"I guess I was right in the end."

"About what?"

"I told you he was a psycho killer." Jessie grinned from ear to ear as she rested her head on Julia's shoulder. "Call me Evelyn! I successfully predicted the future before it actually happened."

"You did."

They sat on the wall listening to the noise from inside. Julia could feel how desperate Jessie was to tell her what she already knew. Even though it was hard, she could at least do this for her daughter.

"I know you want to move out," Julia whispered before kissing Jessie's bonnet. "I spoke to your estate agent. It's okay. I support you."

Jessie's entire body tensed up under Julia's arm, and she didn't say a word. Julia rubbed Jessie's arm to try to bring her out of it, but the silence dragged out.

"You *know*?" Jessie asked finally. "Since when?"

"Since Monday."

"*Monday*?" Jessie cried, pulling back from Julia. "You've known since Monday, and you've let me sweat it out for *five* days?"

"There have been other things going on," Julia reminded her. "I'm not going to pretend like I didn't freak out at first, but Dot made me see sense. I have to let you go, so you can spread your wings and grow into the person you're supposed to be."

"Dot said all that?" Jessie asked sceptically. "Wow."

"She has her moments."

"You're really not angry?"

"Angry?" Julia pulled Jessie back to her side. "Why would I be angry with you? I love you. If you want to move out, then do it, but just know I'll keep your bedroom at home for whenever you want to stay. Even if you move to Timbuktu, it will always be your home."

"I promise not to go to Timbuktu," Jessie said. "But how about the flat above the post office? I can easily afford it, and I really like it. It's mine if I want it, I just need to sign on the dotted line."

"The flat above the post office?" Julia turned and looked across the dark green at the building next to the café. "You'll be able to roll out of bed and get straight to work."

"Exactly." Jessie's voice lightened. "You're still going to see me every day."

"I don't doubt it."

"And I'll still need you to wash my clothes."

"What happened to independence?"

"Baby steps." Jessie winked.

"Speaking of babies, you're not doing this because you feel like you need to because Barker and I might be having a baby, are you? Not that I've asked him yet."

"No," Jessie said firmly. "In fact, that part was a relief. I've been thinking about it for months, but I was scared to upset you. You've done so much for me. I didn't want you to think I was throwing it back in your face. I can do this *because* you've done so much. You gave me a life I never would have had, and now it's my turn to see what I can do with it. Maybe I'll fall on my face, but I need to find out."

"Or maybe you'll soar."

"Or that." Jessie laughed. "I grew up in crammed children's homes and foster homes, then I lived on the streets, and for the past two years, I've been with you. I've never in my whole life known what it feels like to just be me on my own without needing anyone. Not having Alfie and Billy here has given me room to breathe and think about what *I* want, without having to be a sister or a girlfriend. This is what I want. I want to try."

"Then try." Julia clapped her hands. "Sign those

papers first thing on Monday morning and get that ball rolling. Live your life, Jessie, and never be scared to come back to me when you want or need me. I'll always be here."

"Even when you have a screaming baby?"

"Are you kidding?" Julia tittered. "You've just given me a sanctuary above the post office for when I need to get out of the house and leave the baby to Barker. It's the perfect plan. C'mon, should we go back in before Percy's—"

Before Julia could finish her sentence, the fire alarm inside the village hall blared, and the doors burst open. Drenched Victorians ran out, giving Julia and Jessie a glimpse of Percy and Dot on the stage, fanning the burning red curtains as the sprinklers poured down on them.

"And we're back to normal!" Julia exclaimed. "And I wouldn't have it any other way."

"Not quite yet." Jessie nodded to the minibus that was making its way around the village green. "Not if that's who I think it is."

The minibus pulled up outside the church, and a bemused and tanned Brian climbed out as Victorians scattered away from the fire.

"What is going on?" he cried. "I go away for two weeks, and you've all travelled in time? Why do I get the feeling my mother is behind all this?"

"Forget about that!" a squeaky voice called from within the minibus. "Help me out, babe! You know I can't walk without assistance yet."

Brian ran around the minibus and helped Katie out. Along with a beaming tan, she also sported a bright pink leg brace encasing a scaffold of metal pins.

"Nice gear." Jessie nodded. "Hurt?"

"Only when the pills wear off." Katie gave a woozy laugh. "Where's my baby?"

Brian went to find Vinnie, but Katie started to lean like the Tin Woodman. She cried out, and Jessie and Julia dived in, each grabbing an arm to steady her.

"Thanks, girls." Katie wrapped her arms around their necks and kissed them each on the cheek. "I missed you both so much. Thank you for looking after my baby. Was he good?"

"As gold," Julia said.

"Sometimes," Jessie added. "He was okay."

Brian emerged from the crowd with Vinnie in his arms. Apparently forgetting she couldn't walk, Katie dived forward, leaving Jessie and Julia to catch her again.

"He's tripled in size!" Katie wailed as she took

Vinnie into her arms. "Did you miss mama?"

Leaving them to reunite, Julia and Jessie handed Katie over to Brian. Julia joined Barker in front of the open church gates. He clutched her hand in his and kissed it.

"I think I might miss Vinnie," Barker said.

"Really?"

"Yes, I think I might."

"Me too."

"Should we have one?"

"Have what?"

"A *baby*." Barker belly-laughed as he pulled Julia to his chest. "What do you say? The chimney sweep and the maid?"

Julia nuzzled her face into his costume, unsure what to say.

Eventually, she settled on, "Are you being serious right now?"

"Don't you want one?"

"Of course, I want one!" Julia's eyes filled with tears.

"Then let's have one."

"Just like that?"

"Just like that." Barker kissed her on the lips. "I think this party is pretty much over. Why don't we sneak away and start practising?"

Dot burst through, breaking their embrace. Despite the sprinklers, the feathers in her hat were somehow still burning.

"Let me extinguish my gran first." Julia patted him on the backside. "She appears to be a little bit on fire."

As Julia chased her screaming gran around the green, trying to rip off her burning hat, she was fully aware that tonight was the night her life would change forever. With no drama or heartache, they had agreed to have a baby, and Julia couldn't be more excited.

THANK YOU FOR READING &
DON'T FORGET TO REVIEW!

I hope you all enjoyed venturing into Peridale once again!

If you did enjoy the book, **please consider** writing a review. They help us reach more people! I appreciate any feedback, no matter how long or short. It's a great way of letting other cozy mystery fans know what you thought about the book.

Being an independent author means this is my livelihood, and every review really does make a huge difference. Reviews are the best way to support me so I can continue doing what I love, which is bringing you, the readers, more fun adventures in Peridale! Thank you for spending time in Peridale, and I hope to see you again soon!

ALSO BY AGATHA FROST

If you enjoyed *Red Velvet and Revenge*, why not sign up to Agatha Frost's **FREE** newsletter at **AgathaFrost.com** to hear about brand new releases!

You can also find Agatha on **FACEBOOK**, **TWITTER**, and **INSTAGRAM**. Simply search '**Agatha Frost**'.

**The 17th book in the Peridale Café
series is coming April 23rd 2019!** Pre-order
on Amazon now! Just search 'Vegetables and
Vengeance'.

52949352R00205

Made in the USA
Columbia, SC
08 March 2019